A Home Subscription! It's the easiest and most convenient way to get every one of the exciting Coventry Romance Novels! ...And you get 4 of them FREE!

You pay nothing extra for this convenience: there are no additional charges...you don't even pay for postage! Fill out and send us the handy coupon now, and we'll send you 4 exciting Coventry Romance novels absolutely FREE!

SEND NO MONEY, GET THESE
FOUR BOOKS FREE!

CO681

MAIL THIS COUPON TODAY TO:
COVENTRY HOME
SUBSCRIPTION SERVICE
6 COMMERCIAL STREET
HICKSVILLE, NEW YORK 11801

YES, please start a Coventry Romance Home Subscription in my name, and send me FREE and without obligation to buy, my 4 Coventry Romances. If you do not hear from me after I have examined my 4 FREE books, please send me the 6 new Coventry Romances each month as soon as they come off the presses. I understand that I will be billed only $11.70 for all 6 books. There are no shipping and handling nor any other hidden charges. There is no minimum number of monthly purchases that I have to make. In fact, I can cancel my subscription at any time. The first 4 FREE books are mine to keep as a gift, even if I do not buy any additional books.

For added convenience, your monthly subscription may be charged automatically to your credit card.

☐ Master Charge **42101**   ☐ Visa **42101**

Credit Card # _____

Expiration Date _____

Name _____
(Please Print)

Address _____

City _____ State _____ Zip _____

Signature _____

☐ Bill Me Direct Each Month **40105**

This offer expires Dec. 31, 1981. Prices subject to change without notice. Publisher reserves the right to substitute alternate FREE books. Sales tax collected where required by law. Offer valid for new members only.

A SANDITON QUADRILLE

by

Rebecca Baldwin

FAWCETT COVENTRY • NEW YORK

A SANDITON QUADRILLE

Published by Fawcett Coventry Books, a unit of CBS Publications, the Consumer Publishing Division of CBS Inc.

ISBN: 0-449-50187-6

Printed in the United States of America

First Fawcett Coventry printing: June 1981

10 9 8 7 6 5 4 3 2 1

**For Scotti Oliver & James Plumb,
with love & thanks**

AUTHOR'S NOTE/APOLOGIA

The village of Sanditon, Sussex, is the fictional creation of Jane Austen, and adapted to the present story from a novel fragment of that same name, unfinished at the time of Miss Austen's death. It is hoped that the Shade of Miss Austen, together with her many admirers (among which the present authoress humbly includes herself), will indulge the appropriation of this delightful seaside spa as the backdrop for the present tale, and forgive the slight liberties the authoress has taken in embroidering upon the geography and the denizens of Sanditon for her own narrative. It is hoped that the reader will understand that the choice of Miss Austen's locale for this novel was undertaken as much in tribute to the power of that lady's genius of observation as for the irresistible lure of a Regency resort as the natural setting for romantic tangling and untangling.

CHAPTER ONE

Permanent residents of the seaside town of Sanditon had become accustomed to the sight of the couple making their morning stroll on the Strand, but a stranger might steal a second glance at the contrasting pair as they made their way along the seaside walk. Admiral Arkwright was as tall as a mainmast and as round as a grog tub, to use his own phrase, and his habit of retaining the nautical uniform of his retired career only increased his resemblance to his royal crony, Sailor Billy. By contrast, the lady who tucked one gloved hand into the crook of his elbow and balanced a delicate parasol in the other barely reached his shoulder. In her *jeunesse*, the Dowager Lady Rockhall had been known as the Pocket Venus for her small stature and doll-like beauty. Although she was fond of saying that when one passed some fifty summers and became a grandmother, it was time to have done with thoughts of vanity and fashion, her pelisse was in the latest London mode, and a most dashing bonnet was set upon her still-dusky curls. Perhaps most telling of all was the smile that played faintly about the lady's face, for her companion was informing her, as he did at frequent intervals, that she had not lost one iota of her beauty to time, and that he had remained bachelor all of his life for the sake of her fine eyes.

Since Lady Rockhall knew very well that the Admiral had been keeping a voluptuous actress in high style anytime these past twenty years and more, and publicly acknowledged his assistance in the naval careers of his three sons by this female, she could only dip her parasol to hide her smile. But since their friendship had always been predicated about the elaborate charade of his undying love, she made no demur, but shook her head slightly as they passed by a young man riding upon one of the new velocipedes.

"This younger generation!" the Admiral said, shaking his head until his stays creaked. "Risking life and limb upon such a contraption! Steam engines upon a man-o'-war!"

Lady Rockhall watched the retreating machine with interest, wondering just for a second if she would dare to risk life and limb upon such a contraption, for it looked rather interesting, to be able to sail along like so. She shook the thought out of her head. "The Season shall be upon us soon, Henry. I noticed that the Partridges are opening their house." She gave a little sigh of superiority, for she had been a resident of the newly fashionable seaside resort for three years. It suited her needs quite nicely, for while it was not as fashionable as Brighton, it was not as slow as Bath, and the residence of certain of her oldest friends as well as the sea air were highly beneficial to her health. And certainly, for one whose chief pastime since she had retired from

Polite Society was watching people, it was a most interesting place. Perhaps best of all, it was a good three hundred miles from That Woman, as she persisted in calling her daughter-in-law. The two Lady Rockhalls had never gotten along. The Dowager, product of an expansive age and a handsome personal fortune of her own, considered her eldest son's unfortunate choice of spouse to be a toad-eater, an opportunist and a cold-blooded Viper In Her Bosom, and, shortly after the death of the elder Lord Rockhall, had removed herself and all her possessions from the Dower House at Hambly Court, announcing her intention to dwell year-round at her house on the Marine Parade at Sanditon until she was felled with the sea winters rather than remain one more second within the presence of That Woman. Since this plan suited the Dowager very well, she could not help but communicate her situation in terms of the greatest hardship to her bewildered son, with the unhappy result that That Woman had made the break complete between generations.

Lady Rockhall, who had mild contempt for her eldest's timidity, so very different from his dear Papa, missed only her grandchildren, and then only very mildly, for having grandchildren who are almost grown is an unsuitable reminder of advancing age. To console herself for this loss, she sent most spoiling and elaborate gifts at birthdays and Lady Days and Christmas, toys that were certain to destroy the peace of Hambly Court by making a great deal of noise or destruction or both, such as kettle drums and cricket bats, and clothes and fripperies entirely too mature for schoolroom misses. It was a subtle revenge upon That Woman, but her grandchildren adored her for it, and those who were of an independent age communicated with her frequently.

These reflections brought her back to the subject of

her earlier conversation, and without missing a beat she interrupted the Admiral's practiced compliment to return to her original theme.

"Of course I shall be more than glad to have dear Emily visiting with me for the summer. The poor thing must be fagged to death after her London Season. That Woman, I have no doubt, dragged her from pillar to post and back again, as if she were on display at the Bartholomew Fair for the highest bidder! By the tone of her letter, I imagine poor little Emily to be quite worn to the bone. I can only hope that That Woman realizes that she has four more girls to drag out, and that the younger two have a most unfortunate resemblance to their mother!"

"Hey?—Oh, yes Emily!" Admiral Arkwright said, bringing a great deal of concentration to the remembering of Lady Rockhall's eldest granddaughter. Had they been talking about this earlier? he wondered. Something about the girl visiting, and getting herself engaged to one of the Marles. Couldn't be Harry, he'd stuck his spoon in the wall forty years ago, right there at the Coca Tree. Must be his son, or his grandson...

Oblivious to her friend's ruminations, Lady Rockhall continued. "Emily has always been my favorite, of course. Such a gentle, pretty creature! Very much like my late George's mother, with those pale looks and that sweet disposition! All I can say is That Woman had better count herself lucky that Marle took to the girl. She's not likely to snag a viscount for any of the rest of them! Marles are good blood! Of course this one must be nearly thirty—can't recall ever seeing him myself, but they say he's a good catch! Well, I shall be a great grandmother soon!"

The Admiral patted her hand. "There, there, Sophia. Still knock the shine out of all of them!" he assured her bluffly.

10

His reward was a smile that would have put many a younger woman to shame. Lady Sophia Brandywine had never lost that smile. Her small hand on his arm tightened and Lady Rockhall smiled. "But, what was I trying to recall, Henry? It seemed to be particularly important! Well, I daresay Russet will recall. He recalls everything!"

The Admiral nodded. Russet, Lady Rockhall's majordomo, did indeed remember everything, an important attribute when employed by a female as forgetful as her ladyship, who had spent her life leaving behind a trail of books, shawls, gloves and parasols at various stopping points. As a footman, Russet had proved so expert at retrieving his mistress's lost possessions that his late lordship had promoted him to butler. Admiral Arkwright was faintly jealous of Russet, who managed my lady's life and household with skill and style.

Slowly, the couple turned at the end of the Parade and turned for the home journey. Below the stone terrace, several bathing machines had already been dragged to the beach, and one or two truly hearty souls were braving the May sea water.

"If I could but remember what Emily said in her letter," Sophia murmured absently. "There was something irregular about it, but for the life of me, I cannot recall what it was."

"Doubtless it will all be made clear when you see her," the Admiral assured her, gently guiding her into the tea pavilion.

While Sophia nibbled tea and toast, the Admiral put away several cups of thick, creamed coffee laced with brandy and a great number of chocolate rusks. Their conversation was desultory and turned upon the number of summer residents who might be expected to open their houses any day now. The Sanditon Assembly Rooms would be opening with the first dance of the season within the week, and the Admiral had it upon the best authority that both hotels were reserved as full as they could hold through October.

"Still," Sophia said absently, dipping a square of toast into her tea and nibbling thoughtfully, "I wonder if I shall have enough to entertain Emily. After London, she must think us dashed slow, Henry, with only one weekly dance, and a very few private parties. I doubt that she plays whist...."

The Admiral put away a chocolate rusk in one bite and wiped his lips on a napkin. "I'm sure she'll find much to do! Why, there's the Choral Society, if she sings, and most of these modern misses do, and the Assembly on Wednesdays, and sea bathing, and Lord, to judge by the number of sprouts and dandies one may see on the strut all summer, she'll not lack for people to talk to!"

This assured Lady Rockhall to the extent that she was able to persuade herself to order another half slice of toast.

Looking about him at the nearly deserted pavilion, the Admiral leaned forward conspiratorially. "Besides, I have it on good authority that Sailor Billy means to pay us a visit this summer."

Sophia blenched. "Surely he does not intend to bring Mrs. Jordan and all the FitzClarences with him?" she asked in horrified accents. "I cannot and will not have my granddaughter exposed to the *bâtardesse!*"

"Bound to have met 'em all in London," the Admiral said. "They go everywhere! Anyway, m'dear, I understand that Billy has cast Mrs. Jordan off—marrying a German princess to pay his debts!"

Sophia devoured this morsel with far more interest than she had given her toast. "Really!" she whispered. "And what do you suppose Mrs. Jordan had to say about that, after ten children?"

This delicious bit of gossip was discussed for some time and at the sort of length that both the Admiral and Sophia enjoyed, and it was well past noon when her beau finally escorted her to her fine townhouse on Marine Parade. As they made the turn around the Assembly Rooms that separated the Strand from this exclusive residential street, Sophia, shading her eyes with her hand, absently noted that a post chaise was drawn up before one of the houses, and several bandboxes were being handed down from the boot to a waiting footman. It was only when she noted her own green and silver livery that she realized this was her guest.

"Of course! That's what I was trying to recall! Today was the day that Emily was to arrive!" she exclaimed, and quickened her step to a pace the portly admiral was hard pressed to match.

But, as she approached her house, Sophia's brows drew together in a puzzled frown, for the lady standing upon the doorstep in a silk pelisse of celestial blue had a toque of cream and gold braid set upon raven curls, and she was quite certain that Emily was as fair as fair. The lady, drawing off her gloves and conversing with Russet, tossed her head back in a laugh, and Sophia knew it was definitely not Emily's profile, for that was the Brandywine Nose if ever she had seen it on her own face!

Puzzlement descended upon her even farther, and Lady Rockhall stopped dead in her tracks, barely aware of the puffing admiral catching up to her. Now, where, and indeed, who? she thought, and at that most fortunate moment, Russet caught sight of his mistress and correctly judged her expressions. Handing her up the steps with all the stately grace that ought to have belonged to a duke, that tactful servitor ventured a discreet cough. "Miss Miranda Brandywine has come to visit us, Lady Rockhall," he murmured as he gently steered her in the direction of the dark-haired lady.

"Miranda—Brandywine..." Sophia murmured, somewhat cast aback by the feeling that she was squeezing the hand of a vaguely familiar acquaintance.

Miss Brandywine grasped her hand firmly in a glove of York tan. "Dear ma'am, forgive me! I apprehend that I have arrived in advance of my father's letter! The mails are shocking slow these days, and my voyage from Spain was quite swift! We had blue weather the entire way, until, of course, we came into Plymouth, and my maid was shocking sick! I had to leave her in Plymouth until she recovers a bit, but I came post, for a duller place, I have never been!"

Sophia smiled vaguely, nodding at this strange girl with dark eyes and a familiar smile. Now, who? she wondered.

"If you will pardon me for saying so, my lady," Russet intervened, "I was just telling Miss Miranda how marked her resemblance to her father, Sir Francis, has become now that she is a grown lady!"

Confusion momentarily cleared from Sophia's brow, and she made to brush Miss Brandywine's cheek. "My dear Miranda! My dear little niece!" She exclaimed with relief. "But it has been—perhaps ten years since last I set eyes upon you! You have grown into quite a young lady!"

Miranda's dark eyes sparkled with a certain amused intelligence as she received her aunt's embrace. "Not grown, ma'am! As you see, I have inherited the Brandywine stature! Papa says that I am quite a dwarf, and not at all as beautiful as my unfortunate Mama."

"Of course, you are Francis's daughter!" Sophia breathed, relieved to have placed which of her brothers had sent her their offspring. "And where is Francis? Has he returned from France?"

"We were last in Vienna, ma'am! But before that, Spain, yes, for five years! When I left Papa, he was in

14

the devil of a temper, but whether that was caused by me, or by the Treaty, I do not know! Papa is vastly more fond of battle and bivouacs than hotels and negotiations! *Le congrès ne marche pas, mais il danse!*" Miss Brandywine quoted gaily. "So, I suppose that his gout were what made him so out of sorts as to banish me to your doorstep! I hope you do not mind—I would by far rather be exiled to you than to Augusta, for I dislike Bath and pug dogs exceedingly—or at least I did when last I saw them! How odd to be in England again!"

Sophia was enough of a Brandywine to understand the grain, if not the full import, of this enigmatic pronouncement.

The Admiral, huffing slightly, brought himself up the steps just in time to collide with a large trunk being portered into the house. Vaguely, Sophia made him known to her dear brother Sir Francis's daughter Miranda, come to her from Spain, or was it Vienna?

The Admiral, seeing that an afternoon of female conversation and family discussion was in the offing, made his genial inquiries about his old friend General Sir Francis Brandywine, recalled Miranda's late mother as a female of more than surpassing beauty, complimented her daughter, with only the merest shade of untruth upon her inheritance of this fortunate physical asset, and took his leave, planning to stroll up Marine Parade to his own dwelling for the consolation of his cook's excellent luncheon and an afternoon spent at Mrs. Robertson's discreet village. With the *Morning Post* over his face, he would indulge in a comfortable snooze within the cozy embrace of his somewhat irregular domesticity.

In truth, Sophia thought later that afternoon after Miranda had been settled into her bedchamber and allowed to wash off the dust of travel, the girl had not inherited her mother's beauty. But she was passable enough to be called handsome, and there was a certain confident assurance in her demeanor that made her seem a little more mature than her twenty years. That, Sophia shrewdly guessed, was the result of being brought up motherless, and following the drum, for it was easy enough to guess that the girl had received very little in the way of feminine influence under her father's care. Vaguely a governess was mentioned, and a colonel's lady who had chaperoned her through a series of Portuguese villages and garrison towns, but, upon the whole it seemed that Miss Brandywine had always been in charge of herself. And also, Lady Rockhall guessed, had run her father's life and household with all the command the general exercised upon his troops in the field, but with a great deal more tact and diplomacy. She did not press Miranda for answers to her more pressing questions of how and why her niece had suddenly descended upon her, but rather steered the conversation about general family matters and news of the Viennese negotiations, watching in awe while the diminutive young lady managed to eat a large portion of cold beef, several muffins, a bit of asparagus trifle and several raspberry tarts, chattering cheerfully away between mouthfuls.

After Miranda had several times offered her apologies for her unexpected appearance, and had several times been assured that she was quite welcome in her aunt's household, Sophia gently steered the conversation around to the reasons for this unexpected descent.

Miranda buttered the last muffin in the basket and regarded her aunt with sparkling eyes. "I knew I was right to come to you! Dear Aunt Sophia, you were always the most understanding of all my Brandywine aunts! I recall, when I broke the window with the cricket ball that you were so generous in forgiving me!" Dark lashes fluttered mischievously against ivory cheeks, and Miranda leaned forward. "The fact is, Aunt Sophia, Papa has sent me home to regain my senses! I've been exiled in disgrace, until I learn—what was his phrase?—Oh yes! Until I learn dutiful obedience to paternal wisdom! In short, Aunt, I have been cashiered from the service!" The sparkle in Miranda's eyes increased, and Sophia understood this was a retreat, but not a complete rout.

"For, depend upon it, when Papa understands that I am not indulging in a polite little flirtation, that I have quite set my heart upon Charles, he will be forced to cede the battle, if not the war!" Miranda's glossy curls shook a little as she laughed. "It is not at all like Major Drummond. I was only a mere child of seventeen, then, after all, and now I am almost one and twenty— quite old enough to know my own heart!"

"Charles," Sophia repeated, looking about her gold and old rose drawing room as if the papered walls could reveal further details.

Miranda, satiated at last, leaned back in her chair and folded the damask napkin in her lap with a sigh. "Charles," she said dreamily, "is the man I love. Oh, Aunt," she rushed on, taking Lady Sophia's hand in her strong grip. "He is quite unlike anyone I have ever met before, but since all I have ever met are military men like Papa, what else would one expect? Charles is not in the least military. He is sweet, and gentle, and absolutely brilliant! He *invents* things—he is quite a genius! I do think Papa might have come about last month, when Charles demonstrated his gas camping lamp if it had not exploded in Papa's face with such a loud bang when Charles put the firewheel to it! Of course, Charles should have perfected it just a bit more before he presented it to the military, but it is the

17

cleverest idea! And," she added, clasping her hands together against the muslin bosom of her little afternoon gown, "he writes poetry to me!"

"Poetry!" Sophia repeated in hopeless accents, for she was swiftly comprehending Sir Francis's objections to this match.

"Poetry, and quite in the Byronic mode! Or is it Shelley? I am not at all bookish, which is a good thing, for Charles is bookish enough for both of us, and someone must be practical, for even with my mother's annuity, which Papa cannot touch, we shall be forced to reduce our style of living somewhat."

Sophia regarded her simple gown which must have cost all of a hundred guineas and nodded. "And who is this Charles?"

"Oh, Aunt, he is an Adonis! I met him at the Duchess of Richmond's ball, and he was attached to Castlereagh's staff as a secretary, and he has the most beautiful ice-blue eyes, fringed with the longest darkest lashes, and when he compared me to a divine cherubim, and gave me such a look with those pale, pale blue eyes—of course, he is quite unaware of his own looks, which are devastatingly handsome, fine boned and so delicately lovely—" Miranda broke off to sigh, then recollected herself. "His name is Charles Hartley."

"The Hampshire Hartleys?" Sophia inquired in even more hopeless accents, for this clan was well known not to have had a feather to fly with for generations past.

Miranda nodded. "I know, I know, his fortune is so modest as to make the support of a wife quite impossible at present, but when his inventions catch on, as surely they must when he's ironed out one or two very small little flaws in them, we shall be able to live quite respectably. And of course, I have my money. Not that Charles is interested in money—or anything material or military or—worldly. He has to be reminded to eat sometimes! He is so lofty-minded!"

Although Sophia might have expressed it in quite different terms, she tactfully murmured that the Hartleys were frequently given to a sort of otherworldliness and to an artistic nature that required frequent reminders of this material sphere.

"I knew you would be sympathetic!" Miranda said gratefully. "After all, you married Uncle Rockhall for love even though he had not the slightest interest in the military, or making pots of money, or cutting a dash in Society!"

Since Lord Rockhall had been a marquess adequately endowed with both fortune and style, Sophia might have pointed out that the circumstances were entirely different, but she held her tongue and merely nodded, mentally castigating her youngest brother for his lifelong habit of dumping his problems upon her doorstep.

"So, you see," Miranda resumed after her transports upon the thought of Mr. Hartley had ceased, "Papa most strongly objected to Charles, and all because of a silly explosion in the study! I held my line, and let fire my cannons; I should marry Charles or no one! Papa attacked my flank by threatening to lock me in my room until I came to my senses, but since no one else knows how he likes to have his brandy warmed, or exactly how he likes a venison haunch dressed, or how to direct the laundress to starch his socks, he knew that would not serve me, but would end in his capitulation, and the surrender of all his heavy guns! Surprise being the essence of attack, he has decided to divide the ranks by sending me to you, while Charles languishes still in Vienna with odious Lord Castlereagh, who loses patience with him constantly! I may be driven into retreat, but I shall not be defeated! When he sees that I mean to hold this line against siege, he will be forced to call the battle for me!" Her eyelashes fluttered again, and a rather wicked grin crossed her face. "When he sees that he cannot manage without me to run his household, he will negotiate a swift treaty!"

"You and Mr. Hartley mean to make your residence with your father?" Sophia asked faintly.

Miranda nodded. "Only until Charles is well fixed. Then I shall have to cast about for a genteel widow to marry him off to—Papa, I mean, not Charles. There was a colonel's widow from our regiment who lost her husband at Waterloo, and I think when her mourning is over, I shall contrive! They will suit each other very well, for she has always followed the drum and will doubtless give the poor dear some much deserved subordination from the lower ranks!" Miranda licked butter from her fingers most delicately. "So, Aunt, you see where matters stand! But those eyes! Of, if you could but see Charles, I know you would approve!"

Sophia had her doubts about this, but since there seemed little likelihood that she would have the honor, she was able to regard this prospect with complacency.

"Now, I shall not make myself an uncomfortable houseguest, for I am determined not to sink into any of my scrapes while I am under your roof, but rather to be as well behaved and as much assistance to you as possible. I don't sew very well, and I am rather bad at reading aloud, although I did do some theatricals with the other military ladies when I was in Spain, but I am sure that you can find some use for me, running errands or whatever."

Since Sophia paid a large staff of servants exorbitant salaries to perform these duties for her, she was temporarily at a loss to see in what capacity Miss Brandywine tended to offer herself.

But since she had by no means retired from the world, she was able to sketch in what entertainments Sanditon offered.

If Miss Brandywine thought sea bathing, tea parties in the pavilion, the Choral Society and a very slow Assembly once a week to be rather dull after the glittering entertainments of Vienna, she was far too polite to say so, and far too occupied with presenting herself on her best behavior to truly consider how quiet it might be in a little Sussex resort. She was agreeing with alacrity to Sophia's plan of having a little stroll to the Lending Library and the Pump Rooms when Russet appeared in the doorway.

"Miss Rockhall has arrived, my lady!" he announced, only to be unceremoniously thrust aside by a rather tall young lady with pale hair and limpid blue eyes, who tossed aside her muff and bonnet to cast herself, with all the airs of a Tragedy Jill, upon her ladyship's lap.

"Gran'mama!" this female wailed in angst-ridden tones, throwing her arms about Sophia's neck in the embrace of a drowning person. "Oh, Gran'mama, please take me in! I have run away from home! I cannot—I will not!!" She raised great blue eyes to her grandmother's rather startled face. "I will *not* be forced into that Gothic marriage with *him!*"

Absently, Lady Rockhall stroked her granddaughter's head. "Emily," she murmured vaguely. "I quite forgot that you were running away from home! That was what *your* letter said! It was *Francis's* letter that said Miranda was paying a visit! I knew there were two letters—or did I?"

"Two letters, my lady," Russet interjected calmly.

"Well, fancy that!" Sophia remarked. "Is there ought amiss, love?"

CHAPTER TWO

This question, taken together with Miranda's fascinated stare, enabled Emily to gain some control over herself. Still dabbing at tears provoked by her long flight, Emily allowed her grandmother to remove her sadly crushed bonnet and pelisse, and permitted herself to have a few sips from a restorative glass of Madeira, all the while blushing in a most becoming manner as she murmured hesitant apologies for her outburst.

Miranda, who had not seen her cousin in ten years, was generously ready to accede Emily the greater degree of beauty. A pink, English complexion, hair of flaxen gold framing a delicate face and eyes of a far darker blue than those divinely ice-colored orbs of Mr. Hartley all combined to overshadow the fact that Miss Rockhall's dress was slightly out of the mode, and that her bonnet and pelisse had not come from a modiste of the first stare. In short, Miranda thought, assessing her cousin, the girl was of the type who could appear to advantage wearing a grain sack.

She was able to make this evaluation at leisure, for it took several minutes for Emily to be restored to herself. With gently stammered apologies, she took Miranda's hand in her own and presented her cousin with a watery smile. "How do you do, Cousin Miranda? It has been an age—and to be united under such circumstances..." Her voice trailed off, and such color flamed into her cheeks that Miranda felt compelled to give her hand a reassuring pat. "In the general way, I never run on so, but—there are circumstances—"

"Indeed, I am certain there are, cousin! But I am also certain that we may contrive something without very much effort, so if you may compose yourself, and allow your mind to rest, very soon we shall see what can be done."

There was such confidence in Miranda's voice that Emily, for the first time in many weeks, was able to sink back into the chair and close her eyes. The small furrow of tension between her brows smoothed out, and she sighed, "Dearest Miranda, you *always* contrived!"

Sophia, having conferred with Russet and ascertained that one lady could be accommodated in the blue chamber while the other might have the rose, that cook would instantly be informed of the arrivals, that a decanter of Madeira would be sent up, dismissed her servitor to his duties and settled herself in her favorite chair by the hearth, regarding her best-loved granddaughter and her niece. "There! You shall be able to entertain each other! The problem is solved!" she said in tones of relief, and leaned forward to regard Emily most closely. "You looked rather peaked, my dear. Should you wish to see your room immediately?"

Emily shook her head violently. For a second, it seemed as if she would go off again, but Miranda's hand, holding her own tightly, gave her the courage to shake her head. "No, Gran'mama!" She whispered, and balled her handkerchief tightly in her lap.

"Perhaps now, if you are able, you would like to tell us what has happened," Miranda suggested gently, and Emily nodded.

"I have run away from home!" she announced.

"Is that all?" Sophia said in vaguely disappointed tones.

Emily shook her head. "Mama—and Papa, also, for he will do whatever Mama tells him—have consented to my engagement to Lord Marle." She might have been announcing her betrothal to Mrs. Shelley's Monster, so bleak were her tones.

"Marle? Marle. Of course. A very good match. The man has an excellent fortune, one of the best families! I should hate to say it to That Woman's face, but she did quite well with that bit of business, I assure you."

"But you don't understand, Gran'mama!" Emily wailed, "I don't *want* to marry Lord Marle!"

"Is there someone else?" Miranda asked, trying to unravel this tangle.

Emily blew her nose (charmingly, Miranda thought; now *there* was an accomplishment!) and again shook her head. "No, no one. Oh, I had plenty of beaux in London—even Mama said I was a Success, but no one caught my heart. Mama says that people in our position do not marry for love, and that it is imperative that I make a Good Match because Papa's into debt, and there are the rest of the girls to launch off, and I should consider myself very fortunate that Lord Marle offered for me, because he is a viscount, and very rich, and will pay all of Papa's debts, but—" her lips quivered and tears clouded over her eyes, "I don't wish to marry Lord Marle. I wondered perhaps if I thought about it for a while, that the idea would be less—frightening to me,

24

but I thought and I thought and I thought, and I still had nightmares about him, and finally, I decided that I was more afraid of Lord Marle than of even Mama, so I told her how it was, and—and she—well, she did not precisely fly into a passion, but she—she was very angry, and that made Papa angry, and they both flew at my head in such a way, and oh, I could not bear it! So, I came to you, Gran'mama, because I knew that you would not force me to marry Lord Marle!"

A gleam of unholy delight shot through the Dowager's eyes. "Of course, my love," she purred, "you shall stay here and you shall not have to marry Lord Marle, if I have anything to say about it, and I fancy that I have! To throw a spike in That Woman's wheel—well, we shall not say anything about that. But tell me, my love, why are you so frightened of Marle! I have not clapped eyes on him, but I have heard that he was devastatingly handsome, and quite full of style!"

"He frightens me!" Emily wailed. "He looks at one as if—as if he could read one's thoughts, and his love-making is—is quite intense!" Her cheeks flooded crimson, and she dropped her eyes.

"I hope he did nothing improper?" Miranda put in.

Emily shook her curls. "Oh, no, not at all—improper! But he is quite the Corinthian, and he says that when we are married, I shall have to learn to drive to an inch, and ride to hounds, and sail on his yacht—and I am afraid of horses and get seasick! And his house—"

"Runford," Sophia murmured. "An elegant old pile in Hampshire..."

"Runford has forty-eight bedchambers! Queen Elizabeth slept in *two* of them! He says that when we are married, I shall have to preside at table, and manage his houses, and act as hostess for his friends—and his friends frighten me! They talk of politics, and *ton* gos-

25

sip, and such strange things that I can barely keep up with them. I know they must all think I am a great booby, for I am not at all sophisticated, and I am quite terrified of making some gaffe or another and having them all laugh at me for being such a goose! And he says that when we are married, we shall travel, and travel makes me ill—and he is always so abrupt! I could have fainted when Papa said that he had offered for me, for he only danced with me twice, and came to call on us once before he went to see Papa, and I thought that he barely knew I was alive!"

"Sounds exactly like his late father!" Sophia said. "The Runfords were always known for their arrogant manners! It comes from being brought up to believe that you can do no wrong. Family's always been like that, you know. I made my comeout with his aunt—drove a phaeton and four down St. James's Street, and said she could do it because she was a Runford, and Runfords did as they pleased!" Sophia chuckled. "Got away with it, too! But there's not a particle of harm in them, any of them. Arrogant they might be, but fools they ain't! Always great ones for the outdoor life, always great ones to take the dare."

Emily sniffled. "He says that we shall spend a part of our honeymoon in Switzerland, for he wants me to climb mountains! I don't want to climb mountains!"

"Surely there must be something about Lord Marle that you like," Miranda suggested.

Emily frowned. "He has a very nice library," she said doubtfully, "and he said that when we were married, I could buy all the books I wanted." She bit her lips, thinking, while an embarrassed silence descended over the room. "He also introduced me to his family," she added, picking up the threads of her woes, "and they were all as—intimidating as he! I felt like a mouse next to the gods!"

"Dear me," Miranda said practically. "You should never allow yourself to feel that way. Meeting large groups of people—well, Papa says that one may choose his friends, but one isn't responsible for one's family! We have a few loose fish, you konw—Cousin Brandamore—well!"

"His friends are even more frightening than his family. And he is most frightening of all. When he looks at me, I feel ready to melt into the floor, for I know that he's finding yet another fault!"

"If that is the case," Miranda said, "why did he offer for you in the first place? No one forced him to do so."

Emily sniffled, twisting her handkerchief. "He said that he was of an age to be married and provide an heir, and that I was young enough and impressionable enough to be broke to bridle in his style!"

"If Charles said such a thing to me, I should—well!" Miranda exclaimed, rising from her position beside her cousin and pacing the room. "Aunt, I fear Lord Marle is no great paragon of tact—or virtue! Broken to bridle, as if Emily were a mare—"

"A b-brood mare! He says that we must immediately have a child!"

"He does, does he?" Miranda flared. "I have not met this man, and I pray for his sake that I never do, for I think I should lay my crop across his shoulders! Any blind fool with a thimbleful of experience with women would immediately understand that you are the sweetest of females, cousin, and one of the most obliging girls in the world! But I think he takes advantage of you here! Aunt, you cannot countenance such an engagement! Would you have poor Emily broken to bridle like an untamed horse?"

"I can't?" Sophia repeated blankly. "Oh, no—I cannot! You are quite, quite right, my dear! It would never do! The man has thrown Emily into hysterics. Of course, he's a Runford, and that would explain it, but if Emily feels strongly about it—"

"I do!" Emily announced, clasping her hands to her bosom. "I really do! I would rather die than marry him!"

"I don't think you need make that choice," Miranda said mildly. "But I am beginning to understand your situation! Perhaps in time Aunt Rockhall will see that this will not do. I daresay there must be a hundred gentlemen most anxious to speak to your father."

"Perhaps," Emily said naively, "but they never had the chance! *He* was right there! I never had such a miserable thing as a Season in my whole life!"

"Well," Sophia said, rising from her chair and putting a gentle arm on both of the girls shoulders. "I shall write to That Woman and tell her that you are staying with me. Whatever hysterics she may have, whatever motive she might have in auctioning you off like a slave, you are safe here. Even That Woman would not dare to tangle with me, here in my own home!"

"Thank you, Gran'mama," Emily said gratefully, blowing her nose.

Lady Rockhall nodded. "Well, now, it is coming on to be time for my afternoon nap. Dear me, what an afternoon! At least you two will be able to provide company for one another." She shook her head. "And I thought I should have a very dull summer."

After her dresser had brushed out her hair and tenderly covered her mistress with a satin comforter, Sophia stretched out upon her chaise lounge and meditated upon the view of the sea from her window. In her experience, nothing could be more disastrous than poets with ice-blue eyes and long black lashes. She wondered how Francis ever managed to put his foot down with little Miranda. She was so much the Brandywine...quite unlike poor Emily, who exhibited a great many of the present Lord Rockhall's somewhat

28

bookish characteristics. Emily was the sweetest, most biddable girl in the world, and Lord only knew where she had summoned the courage to confront That Woman—Lord Marle must be a monster indeed, for the chit to rise to such courage. Well, that would not do, either.... what was it she was supposed to do when she awoke from her nap? She had already forgotten as she dozed off.

"Ice-blue eyes," Emily was sighing at that moment, watching as Miranda competently removed her few sadly crushed dresses from her portmanteau and hung them in the wardrobe.

Her cousin nodded. "Ice blue and the longest, darkest lashes, as you may see by that miniature. Hayter did it up, so it's more a fashionable likeness than a true one, but Charles is quite handsome, and Papa is being truly unreasonable...." Miranda held a sprig muslin up against her waist and laughed at the trailing hem. "What a dwarf I am next to you, Cousin Emily! If I were only more attractive, perhaps I could become the second Pocket Venus!"

Emily closed the miniature case reluctantly and handed it back to Miranda, who slipped it around her neck. "Don't let Gran'mama hear you say so! She's very proud of that title, you know!"

Miranda smiled and nodded, turning from the *armoire* to seat herself on the edge of Emily's bed. Emily, lying down to recover her strength with a cold cloth pressed to her temples, gave her cousin a wan smile. "But you have changed too, Miranda. You've grown up to become quite beautiful."

Miranda shook her head. "No, I shall never aspire to those lofty heights, for you, my love, are quite the most lovely creature I ever saw in my life! And to think what a pair of haggle-straggle girls we were when last we met! I had spots, and you were inclined toward embroidering the afternoons away while I was out breaking windows with a cricket bat!"

To judge by their giggles, they might still have been little girls, as they recollected their childhood adventures.

"It seems so very long ago," Emily sighed at last, closing her eyes. "And now, you are in a tangle and I am in another!"

"We are both having our romantic problems, as Miss Tilter used to say," Miranda recalled her old governess. "Romantic problems."

"But you are so confident of a happy ending, and I am not," Emily said wanly.

"Never you mind, my love! There must be thousands of men out there dying to make your acquaintance. You'll find someone you can love, never you fear."

"It must be very nice to be in love," Emily whispered, a hint of longing in her voice.

Miranda shrugged. "I am not precisely the most romantic person to ask. I saw Charles, and I knew that was for me, and that was that. Those ice-blue eyes..." She shrugged. "Anyway, it is a bit of a strange feeling. It's...not quite what I thought it would be like. I thought, you know, that when you were truly in love that you never felt out of sorts or impatient with the other person...but Charles and I sometimes can't seem to agree about things..." Miranda's voice trailed off.

"But I suppose that you find compromises...surely, he must be rather firm, to invent wonderful things and write you poetry must indicate a character of great creativity—you must allow for that—"

"Oh, Charles eventually sees things my way," Miranda said cheerfully. "Should you like to go and have a look at the bathing machines? I declare, I am dying to try out this new exercise!" Emily gave a delicate shudder and closed her eyes. "Not at this moment, thank you...I feel so exhausted from the trip...."

Miranda raised one eyebrow in a quizzical way. Having traveled twice the distance of her cousin in half the time, she was still ready to sally forth and view what Sanditon had to offer. But she smiled and patted her cousin's hand in quite the old way. "You rest, my dear. You've had a very exhausting day, I'm certain...one may stroll, no doubt, upon the beach without a maid or footman in attendance, but oh, what would I give to ride my horse through that surf...."

Emily nodded, already half-asleep.

Miranda rose to go to her own room, touching the miniature about her neck. Dear Charles, she thought somewhat wistfully, if you only knew what I am doing for the sake of your fine eyes. She smiled to herself.

CHAPTER THREE

It was an hour to teatime when the cousins finally ventured abroad. Walking arm in arm with her cousin as they dutifully admired the fine hand of Nash upon the neat row of homes lining the Strand, Miranda was satisfied that they offered the interested viewer a fine study in contrasts. Emily, so tall and fair, was, to her cousin's fond eye, breathtakingly beautiful in a white muslin walking dress trimmed with hems of Russian lace and a rose-pink spencer which matched the ribands adorning her chipstraw bonnet, while Miranda's Paris promenade gown of lilac cambric, closely banded in the new mode with deeper shades of mauve, her dark curls accented by a smart little cap of silk and grosgrain, certainly made her appear to the best advantage.

Sanditon was still thin of company that early in the season, but even this was worked, in Miranda's mind, to their benefit, for as they strolled along the Marine Parade, peering into the shop windows, she was quite aware that these two new and interesting arrivals were attracting admiring glances from certain of the permanent inhabitants of the resort. Perusing the volumes for rental at the library, they made their selections with half an ear open for the local gossip of impending arrivals and were feminine enough to be gratitified by the interesting observation of one clerk to another that several gentlemen had registered their names with that establishment in anticipation of escaping the London heat by the Sussex coast. Miranda was not at all bookish, and her reading selections inclined toward novels of a not very elevating sort, but Emily was happy to browse for half an hour bearing away several titles of poetry, a natural history of the ocean, and a learned commentary upon the works of Plato.

This last volume caused Miranda to tease her cousin lightly as they left that worthy establishment to continue their stroll past the Sanditon Assembly Rooms, where a playbill announced the impending performance of a concert of Haydn. "Take care, dear cousin, that everyone does not get into the idea that you are a bluestocking, reading Plato."

Emily, whose mood had been restored to its natural sunniness until that moment, suddenly clouded over. "That is exactly what Lord Marle says. He, of course, had the benefits of a Cambridge education, and now confines his reading to sporting journals and lists from marine outfitters. He feels that action is more important than reflection...."

Miranda, uncomfortable in the twin circumstances of finding herself in agreement with Lord Marle and having caused her beautiful cousin distress, swiftly exerted every degree of her personality to restore her cousin's spirits, finally succeeding in distracting her attention to the large number of fashionable vehicles to be seen in the courtyard of the Sanditon Hotel, which must certainly give credence to the library clerk's remarks upon the number of gentlemen holidaying by the seaside.

At the end of the Marine Parade, they gazed with some awe upon the Royal Duke's Theatre being erected by a gang of burly workmen, and mourned that the building would not be completed in time to give performances this season, but agreed that it would certainly be an edifying spectacle when completed, with the innovation of the new system of gas-lighting. Upon this subject, Miranda was able to enlighten her cousin with all of her beloved Charles' observations and experiences, and the good-natured Emily naively commented upon her increasing respect for such an enterprising man of progressive genius. "For, from what I have observed in London, machines will soon provide us with every convenience," she said as they strolled over the sandy hills toward the old fishing village that had originally comprised all of Sanditon.

Miranda nodded, quite in charity with her cousin for these admiring views. "Oh, Charles is quite brilliant, but I mean to make certain—once we are married, you know, that he turns his mind toward more practical matters. Progress is all very well in its place, but really, one can and must survive in the world—" She did not see the strange, sidelong glance her cousin delivered from beneath the rim of her little parasol.

The old village of Sanditon was quite in contrast to the modern; in place of the broad classical Regency facades and gleaming white paint, it was comprised of ancient stucco and wood dwellings, either single story or at the most two flights with heavy wooden shutters protecting doors and windows from ocean gales. Strolling through the narrow streets which meandered across the dunes, their fancy was caught by the use of ship's timbers and outfittings incorporated into the general design of these little landbound erections. A careful wending down the High brought them to the chandleries and cooperies and boatyards, where the air was thick with the atmosphere of tar, hemp and the pungent scent of exotic woods.

Miss Brandywine, who knew something of boats, and long inured to the stares of the curious by a childhood spent in Portuguese villages, strolled upon the quay, admiring the trim boats, moored at their slips, but Emily, raised in a more sheltered environment, protested uneasily that they were being *stared at dreadfully*, and that boats reminded her of Lord Marle's yacht, and that the thought of the yacht made her seasick.

Slightly amazed at her cousin's sensibility, Miranda allowed Emily to guide her away from the boatyards and back along the beach toward the new town.

"If everything reminds you of Marle," Miss Brandywine said, "then you are never going to able to venture out of your bedchamber."

Miss Rockhall shuddered, turning large eyes upon Miss Brandywine. "I know I must sound goosish to you, Miranda, for you are not afraid of anything, but—if only you could understand!"

"I understand only too well," Miranda replied, linking her arm into Emily's and lifting her face to the sea breezes and the sound of the circling gulls. "And I assure you, Emily, all it takes is a little firmness. You should immediately inform Lord Marle that your engagement was a tragic mistake, and that would both be better to search elsewhere for a partner!"

Emily shook her head. "I cannot—I dare not! Mama would—"

Miranda's patience was short. "This for your Mama!" she exclaimed snapping her fingers. "If you write to Lord Marle, and cry off, there is nothing your Mama can do about it! I am certain that not even Aunt Rockhall could force you to marry against your will—"

"I am not very brave, Miranda," Emily said gently.

"Yes, but you have Aunt Sophia's protection! And I daresay Aunt Rockhall would never dare to cross swords with *her!* We shall compose a very civil note this very evening, and you will be able to rest easy that even an ogre like Marle would not be so ungentlemanly as to allow the engagement once he understands that you feel you would not suit!"

Such was Miranda's confidence that Emily was assured, and her spirits much elevated. She was able to turn her attention toward the variety of seashells lying on the dreck line, collecting the prettiest of these to assemble into a collage for her little sisters still at home.

Miranda, who thought that seashells were all very well and good in their place, which was upon the beach, watched Emily with a vague sort of indulgence, already composing that very civil little note in her head.

Arriving back at Sophia's just before teatime, they were both gratified to learn that Mr. Theobald, the Master of Ceremonies of the Sanditon Assembly Rooms, had come to leave his card upon them and urge Lady Rockhall to place her granddaughter and niece's names upon the rollbook for membership.

Since Mr. Theobald had described them as jewels that were certain to ornament the coming season, they were prepared to be quite in charity with this elderly gentleman, and beneath Sophia's indulgent gaze, managed, each in her own way, to thoroughly charm him through the tea and cucumber sandwiches, in such a way that he was able to take back the report that Miss Rockhall and Miss Brandywine were belles of the first order, young ladies of grace and accomplishment and

36

precisely the sort of *ton* he wished to attract to the Assembly Rooms.

This not unnaturally aroused some curiosity in the breasts of those who had not been privileged to observe these two upon their exploratory walk about the town, and when, after dinner, Sophia prevailed upon them to accompany her to the Pump Room for a glass of the odiously brackish and bracingly healthy waters, they were gratified to find Mr. Theobald beforehand in presenting them to a variety of gentlemen. Since most of these individuals were of an age with their fathers, it being that early in the season, their hearts were not in any perils of being immediately lost, but their dance cards for Wednesday night were desirably full, and they were able to retire to the Strand with the assurance that they had, as Sophia proudly said, cut a dash.

"For depend upon it my loves, when the Corinthians and the bucks come down from London, you shall already be established over all the other young ladies!" she declared.

Emily indulged her grandmother in a hand or two of whist before bedtime. Since she was not a good player and Sophia was able to trounce her roundly, her gran'mama sailed off to her own chamber in excellent spirits, leaving the cousins to the field.

Emily played rather moodily upon the pianoforte, pausing from time to time to gaze out upon the crashing surf, while Miranda settled herself at the writing desk to the art of composition. She tore up several sheets and crossed out several lines before she was finally satisfied with the results. Rising from the rosewood secretary, she handed the sheet to Emily without a word, but hovered over her for a critique.

Emily's hand trembled as she took the fatal sheet, but she read it aloud in a clear voice.

* * *

"'My Dear Lord Marle,

Although I cannot help but be sensible of the great honor you have done me to propose we'—what is that word, Miranda, there—oh, I see, *'unite'* in marriage, upon Reflection, I cannot help but feel that my Honor impels me to inform you that I have become convinced that we should not suit one another within the state of Holy Matrimony. Our differences are so vast that I feel not even my abiding respect for you could close the Chasm which lies between your Station and mine, and to carry on further with this Engagement would be Tragic for both of us. If you would give your consideration to these matters, I am certain that you must agree. In hopes that we shall e're remain Friends, if not Spouses, I am Your Most—'" Emily broke off. The paper trembled again in her fingers, and she shook her head. "Oh, Miranda, he will be furious! He is so—very proud!"

"Arrogant, you mean," Miranda said firmly, guiding her cousin to the writing table and placing the pen in her hand. "Now you just copy out what I have written and there will be an end upon the matter."

"Perhaps I should consult with Gran'mama," Emily said doubtfully. "It hardly seems right to—"

"Are you always going to let other people dictate your life, cousin?" Miranda asked, pushing a blank sheet before her. "It is your fate which is being determined here, and even your grandmother thinks Marle is a good catch! No, my love, you do as I say, and think no more upon it; we shall mail the letter tomorrow and that will be the end of it."

With a little sound in the back of her throat, Emily copied out Miranda's scrawling handwriting in her own precise characters and added her signature with a little sigh. "Oh, it is done! I cannot believe it! I feel so free!" she exclaimed, leaning back in the chair, grasping at Miranda's sleeve.

Miss Brandywine smiled and nodded. "And already you look so much better, my love! So, you see, it only takes a very little effort to manage one's own affairs. There, the matter is done with, and you shall have to think no more upon it." As she spoke, Miranda folded the sheet and sealed it with a bit of wax. As Emily gave it the address of his lordship's estate, Miranda nodded, brushing a curl away from her face. If nothing else, she reflected, she had at least salvaged this visit by persuading her cousin to alter a step that might have ruined her life.

Still feeling very proud of herself, she picked up the brace of candles and guided them up the stairs to their beds.

But while Miranda slept and dreamed of her Charles, Emily lay awake in the darkness, listening to the roll of the surf outside her window. The night watch made his rounds three times before she was able to drop into an uneasy sleep; and even then, her dreams were punctuated with visions of Lord Marle, risen up in the terrible anger of his pride, descending upon the Strand to kidnap her away in his yacht.

Miss Rockhall may not have been a reader of the Gothic tales which Miss Brandywine enjoyed so much, but she did not need their stimulus for her own vast imagination.

But when Emily awoke in the morning, she felt a curious sensation of having a heavy weight lifted from her shoulders, and at the breakfast table, she managed to be quite gay. Perhaps the calm way in which Miranda buttered her third slice of toast and poured a second cup of strong black coffee reassured her that indeed everything would be all right. Miranda had always managed to relieve her of the worst scrapes of childhood, taking the blame upon her own defiant shoulders and avoiding anything worse than a stern lecture from her father, a diatribe which would have sent Emily into spasms of guilt, but only managed to briefly curb her cousin's adventures before she was off again into some new and even more dangerous scheme.

Promptly at ten, the Admiral came calling upon Lady Rockhall. At first, he was a little inclined to feel jealousy toward the younger generation, certain that they would lay claims to the company that he considered his own exclusive right, but when he determined that the ladies had business of their own and intended to part company with Sophia and himself at the Marine Parade, he relaxed slightly and offered up his opinion that sea bathing was precisely the thing to be of the greatest benefit to the health and well-being of younger people, and abjured them to try it at once.

Promising that would be their immediate intention once they had seen to their errands, Emily and Miranda made their way to the Sanditon Hotel, where Miranda posted not only Emily's letter to Lord Marle, but one of her own to Mr. Charles Hartley. Emily was a little shocked that Miranda would carry on anything so highly improper as a clandestine correspondence, but assumed that Miranda's manners were more continental than her own, and held her peace.

It was therefore with the greatest goodwill that the two ladies descended the beach to the bathing machines. Miranda was all afire to submit herself to the ministrations of sea air and salt water, but Emily was more hesitant, for the surf, to her eye, looked rather dangerous, and the air was still, she feared, a little chill.

But Miranda was able to persuade her to divest herself of her garments within the safety of the bathing machine and adapt the long, loose gown and mobcap required to submit oneself to the waves.

Giggling at the appearance they must make in their

shrouds and caps, the two girls allowed the sturdy attendant, a portly female named Mrs. Gunn, attired in the black shroud and scarf of her occupation, to submerge them in the water before the machine, enduring her sturdy homilies of the healthful benefits to be obtained from a brisk exercise in the ocean's waters. Emily was content to stand in lapping surf up to her knees, but Miranda essayed a swim out beyond the breakers; encumbered as she was by yards of material, she could only manage a few strokes and the stern approbation of Mrs. Gunn.

After an hour or so of this treatment, Mrs. Gunn sternly called them out of the water and into the bathing machine where they toweled themselves off and dressed again, pronouncing sea bathing a most agreeable pastime, and one that must be repeated.

From the bathing machines, they retired to the tea pavilion where bracing mugs of Earl Gray and several croissants apiece restored their energy. One or two of their elderly beaux from the Pump Room stopped by their table for a few moments of conversation, and Miranda was able to ascertain that hacks could be hired from the hotel livery stable. She politely refused the offer of her particular gallant to procure her an animal, much shocking him by pronouncing that her father had always advised her to choose her own mounts, but Emily was intrigued by the information that donkey rides were available for those who cared to be led along the edge of the beach by attendants.

In this manner, they were able to pass their afternoon until teatime, after which Emily and Sophia repaired to their chambers for a rest before dinner and the Assembly.

Miranda's maid, a dour-looking Portuguese female of indeterminate age and fierce devotion to her mistress, had arrived, so in company with this person,

Miranda set off for the Sanditon Hotel where she was disappointed to find that the London mail had brought her no letters from Vienna. Charles, Miranda decided with a little sigh as she contented herself with the purchase of two pairs of silk stockings and a hat she knew would look far better on Emily than herself, was forgetful again. But she nonetheless spent five guineas to console herself and returned home with a small crease between her brows.

Maria, whose loyalty to her mistress did not preclude her from sharing Sir Francis's opinions about Miss Brandywine's beloved, summarily ordered her to recline upon the chaise, which Miranda meekly did in a way that would have surprised anyone who did not know that good dragon had been with her all of her life. As she dutifully reclined, Miranda was diverted for three quarters of an hour by Maria's sullen Portuguese comments upon the horrors of traveling in a Protestant Barbarian country, Miranda's own inability to maintain her wardrobe by the standards which she had been taught, the woeful lack of sophistication to be found among servants in England and the necessity of polishing her mistress's jewels in anticipation of a gathering which would in no way ever begin to rival the glittering balls of Vienna, at which, to hear her tell it, Miranda had been the major adornment. Nonetheless, she managed to have her mistress bathed and dressed before the dinner hour, and with a grudging snort that ill concealed her pride in her own handiwork and her affection for her young charge, turned Miranda about before the pier glass.

Miranda's dark curls were brushed into the style known as the méduse about her face; her ball dress, one of her more conservative, was a delicate confection of celestial blue chiffon over an underskirt of silver taffeta caught at hem and sleeve with tiny embroidered silver birds. About her neck, she wore her mother's sapphire pendant, and droplets from the same stone were fastened to her ears. A champagne fan, all the rage in Vienna, was depended from her arm and her delicate silver sandals placed upon her feet. She was engaged in the act of trying to draw on her gloves while Maria attempted to adjust a silver gossamer shawl about her shoulders when Emily timidly entered the room.

At the sight of Miranda's stylish ensemble, her cousin uttered admiring phrases, but Miranda could not help but feel that Emily, in a voile dancing dress in a delicate shade of pink with tiny cap sleeves and a delicate tracery of seed pearls running down the deeper pink bands in front, her blond hair spilling over her ears in glorious profusion and only the most delicate of pearls clasped about her throat, needed no other ornament to set her off to perfection. But she would not have been Miranda had she not pulled an embroidered Indian shawl from her own wardrobe to present to her cousin when the color matched so perfectly with the pink of her dress, or carelessly delivered into that young lady's astounded hands the caplet she had purchased that afternoon with what would have been, for Emily, a quarter's pin money, proclaiming that it made her look like the little drab she was, but set off the taller girl to true advantage.

Having assured one another that they would be able to make their first public debut in Sanditon Society without fear of being chided for drabs, the cousins went down to dinner arm in arm.

Lady Rockhall, in a ballgown of mauve net with several plumes in her hair, watched with approval as her charges made up one set after the other. Since there were a great many gentlemen present who had been her assiduous courtiers in her youth, she herself did not lack for partners, but felt in this role of chaperone that it might be best to confine her activities to a sedate boulanger with the Admiral, who hung at her elbow all evening, glaring at the rest of her gallants from beneath his heavy eyebrows.

Since the season was still early, there were not as many guests present as Mr. Theobald might have wished, but he was able to congratulate himself that my lady's young females had caused quite enough interest to make the evening a success. The sudden and somewhat mysterious arrival of two young persons in Sanditon had caused a certain degree of comment and interest, and a goodly proportion of genteel Sanditon had turned out to meet the pair. Later on in the summer, he knew, the arrival of more young persons would abate such gratifying attentions to a single pair of ladies, no matter how attractive—and *mon dieu,* he must admit that the fair Miss Rockhall was a diamond of the first water. It was only a great shame that she was known to be the fiancée of Viscount Marle. The dark Miss Brandywine, however not so beautiful, was certainly dashing and very much in the continental fashion, and, he added to himself, was known to be an heiress of considerable fortune. *Alors,* it would be an interesting summer. Perhaps he might even introduce the waltz this year, since Miss Brandywine assured him it was all the rage in Vienna. It would certainly put him a cut above Mr. Almack, to be the first to have the waltz danced in his assemblies!

When, precisely at the stroke of midnight, the orchestra laid aside its instruments and the ladies and gentlemen began to gather to leave, Miss Rockhall was rather glad to be released from the dancing, but Miss Brandywine was slightly incredulous, for she was just beginning to catch her feet, as she put it.

44

Perhaps it was only to be expected that a female of a somewhat retiring nature, raised up on quiet country assemblies and dancing parties in the homes of people she had known all her life, whose shyness had made the whirl of a London season exhausting and often terrifying, would find the Sanditon Assembly a bit of an ordeal; for being faced with so many new people, so many names to recall and with so many of her Mama's strictures upon her conduct engraved upon her mind, her retiring disposition could be severely taxed.

By contrast, Miranda, who had cut her social teeth at the famous ball given by the Duchess of Richmond in Brussels and had danced through many a pair of shoes in Vienna, living on champagne and boundless energy to dance until four in the morning and still be able to have her morning ride at nine, found the entertainment a trifle flat. There was no waltz to set off her tiny figure and her fashionable gowns, no international coterie of gentlemen whose conversation and wit matched her own, none of the political and military talk upon which she thrived, no intrigues and amours upon which to speculate in quite a naughty fashion, and no champagne. Lemonade and country dances— well, really! Nonetheless, she had managed to indulge in one or two very harmless flirtations with gentlemen old enough to claim her father as a boyhood friend, and had restrained herself from any sort of conduct that would have shocked these staid English dowagers, always so ready to condemn, and tactfully pronounced the evening most interesting. Let Sir Francis receive *that* report in Vienna!

Feeling the novelty of piety, she was content to retire to her bed with her aunt and cousin at the hour of one, and was soon fast asleep, for her military training had allowed her the luxury of snatching repose whenever and however she could.

Emily, whose neurasthenic character was always overstimulated by the ordeal of social gatherings, sought to lull herself into her bed, a cold cloth upon her forehead, a single candle illuminating the page; she studiously pursued the tidal currents of the world's oceans, awaiting sleep with precisely the degree of anxiety that made it the most elusive.

She had finally reached the point where she believed that if she snuffed the candle and laid upon her back for fifteen minutes, breathing in rhythm and counting sheep, she might fall off, when a curious sound was carried over the gentle swell of the breakers to her ears. Puzzled, Emily laid aside the book, frowning as she tried to discern this unexpected intrusion into her peace. It was certainly the music of a guitar, she decided, and the low harmony of a male voice raised in gentle and not unpleasant song.

Curiosity finally overcame trepidation, and Emily pushed aside the bed covers and padded to the window which overlooked the back garden. She parted the curtains and peered into the darkness below.

Illuminated in the waxing moonlight, she was surprised to see a young man with an instrument, gazing up toward her window as he raised his voice in a French song.

For a single second, Emily was transfixed. The gentleman, and gentleman he must be, to judge by the cut of his clothes, seemed, in the moonlight, to be the shade of which dreams are made. His fine-boned face framed by dark brutus curls, raised toward her own, seemed to be that of an angel. The delicate music he coaxed from his instrument was nothing more than a celestial accompaniment.

Despite her Mama's training, there still lurked romantic visions within Emily's soul, and she was touched by the *chanson,* which compared the singer's love to the moon, the sun, the stars, the roses of June and a great many other desirable objects.

Entranced by the moonlit scene, Emily leaned against the sashes, entranced. Had she known that the candlelight behind her outlined her silhouette rendering her person, if not her identity, visible to the serenader, she might have withdrawn in horror at being espied in her nightdress by a strange young gentleman, no matter how handsome, or how romantic the scene.

With one last sigh, the music of the guitar died away. The young man bowed, laid his instrument against the stone bench and gazed upwards.

"I have come!" he announced simply, and with a bound, seized the heavy branches of the ivy which clung to the wall and began to ascend toward the window with an admirable dexterity, finding hand and footholds in the ancient vinery as he gazed upwards at a rather startled Emily.

It occurred to her that she might arouse the household, or at least seize the poker from the hearth, but fortunately Emily did neither. The object closest to hand was a slender volume of poetry, and she snatched that up, clutching it to the bosom of her nightdress, entirely too enchanted with the angel's grace and audacity to do much more than admire the grace of his ascent toward her window.

"Nothing could stop me," he rather breathlessly declared as he attained that goal, "for I knew that I would—I *must* see you, my love!"

For one terrible second, it occurred to Emily that this might be a ruse of Lord Marle's, that the fatal letter had, by some devious treachery, reached his hands far too soon and brought him to this revenge. She uttered a little squawk and drew back a step as the young man, not without an easy grace, clambered over the window. "Actually, serenading, and climbing an ivy vine are a little more difficult in the execution than the planning—" the young man whispered softly as he placed himself in the windowsill, huffing slightly with his exertions. "But nothing would deter me from the female I love—"

In the dim light of the single candle, Emily and the young man stared at one another, mouths agape.

"You are not Miranda," the young man announced simply, his tone rather implying some cosmic mistake than embarrassment.

"And you are Charles Hartley!" Emily exclaimed, pressing a hand over her mouth as she recognized the ice-blue eyes which sent her cousin into raptures.

They regarded one another for several seconds, each one absorbing this woeful truth with something less than the dread circumstances might have dictated.

Emily was conscious of the impression that Mr. Hartley was rather handsomer than his miniature, and that there was about him a certain rather careless, Shelleyan air of not being quite of this world, for despite his climbing exertions having done a certain amount of disarrangement to his person, no gentleman with his mind entirely upon the realities of the material world would have selected a plum-colored waistcoat to wear with a snuff brown coat, and his cravat left much to be desired in the careless style in which it had been knotted. Rather than repulsing her, these minor infractions of *ton* rather charmed Emily, and she was surprised to find herself disarmed by a smile as naive and sweet as it was unexpected.

"No," she heard herself whispering, "I am Miranda's cousin Emily Rockhall. At least you have the correct house, if not the correct room."

"Ah." Mr. Hartley nodded, still smiling. "Fair maid by candlelight—if only I had pen and paper to jot down the poetry you inspire for me, Miss Rockhall—" Carelessly, he swung himself into the room, and Emily was surprised to find herself gazing directly into those eyes. Since she was used to being somewhat above the height of many gentlemen, this was indeed a pleasant sensation. "Fair Miss Rockhall, when taken unawares, how like a goddess thou are to me—" Mr. Hartley murmured, patting his pockets and producing a notebook, but no writing implement. "Can you recall those lines? I would so much appreciate it, for I find myself without the means to inscribe the poem which rises to my mind...." He shrugged helplessly and gave her his devastating angelic smile. "But I see you are holding Byron!"

"What?" Emily whispered, much shocked. "Oh, I see, you mean the book—"

"Sometimes an excellent poet, but not to compare with Shelley," Mr. Hartley said absently, settling himself on the edge of the windowsill and carelessly brushing ivy leaves from his hair.

"I think I must agree with you," Emily replied, quite unaware of the impropriety of discussing poetry in her bedchamber with a strange young man at the watch hours of the morning. "Shelley it seems to me is possessed of much finer feelings than Byron could ever aspire to! Of course, Mama quite forbids me to read either poet, she says they lead most improper lives, but what is one's life to one's art?"

Charles Hartley nodded. "Exactly, dear ma'am! I have often said so myself. But I could never offer a lady anything less than the most conventional of arrangements—" As he placed a hand upon his heart, Emily noted that there was a large rent in the arm seam of his coat.

"Perhaps I should go and fetch Miranda. She is asleep in the next room," Emily said swiftly, suppressing the urge to fetch needle and thread.

49

"Miranda!" Mr. Hartley sighed. "Yes, Miranda! Tell me, is she well? Does she feel herself to be in exile? Miranda, most delicate, most sensitive of females! She is a fragile goddess, as light as the dew upon the morning grass," Mr. Hartley rhapsodized passionately. "I must see her! It was for her sake that I have come here."

"Yes, of course," Emily said, deeply touched by such devotion. "I shall go and awaken her at once!"

But Miranda, upon being awakened from a sound sleep, seemed anything but touched by this proof of her lover's devotion. Knotting the cord of her dressing gown about her waist, she muttered angrily to Emily's shocked ears. "Good Lord, has he gone mad? If word of this reaches Sir Francis, nothing will move him to consent to our marriage! Good God, why did he not simply awaken the household?"

With Emily trailing along behind her, a little shattered at this most unromantic reaction to the sudden appearance of her cousin's beloved, Miranda stalked into the other bedchamber.

"Charles my dearest, how *could* you?" Miranda demanded, standing on tiptoe to peck at her lover's cheek. "Serenading my cousin and climbing vines—it's a small miracle you did not choose my aunt's room, and then there would be a fine mess indeed! Whatever shall we do when Sir Francis finds you've taken French leave in Vienna? He will never agree to our marriage if he finds out about this, and you must remember, for I explained it to you very carefully, that it was necessary for both of us to act with the strictest propriety to convince him that ours was to be a stable relationship—"

Emily, a silent witness to this, wondered how Mr. Hartley could describe her practical cousin as a creature of morning dew, but Mr. Hartley merely smiled and took the small hand that was angrily pointing a finger at his person. Indeed, he towered over his beloved, Emily noted, and might as easily have picked her up into his arms as a doll. But he did not, merely lowering his eyes and looking for all the world like a repentant schoolboy, as he caught up the accusatory hand within his own two and pressed it against his lips, which somewhat melted Miss Brandywine's wrath.

"But my dearest love, I did not take French leave!" Mr. Hartley said in the silence this produced. "Lord Castlereagh dismissed me!"

Miranda sank into a chair, regarding Mr. Hartley with horror. "Oh, *no!*" She whispered. "Charles, what did you do? Oh, no, our chances are completely ruined, for depend upon it, Sir Francis will never capitulate now!"

Mr. Hartley had the grace to look a little sheepish. "All I really did was demonstrate to Prince Metternich the benefits of my system of gas-lighting—"

Miranda rose from her chair and paced about the room, the heavily embroidered folds of her robe sweeping the floor. "Oh, Charles, how *could* you?" she demanded. "Not Metternich! Anyone else but him! Good Lord, my darling, what devil possessed you to do such a thing?" Despite herself, her lips trembled with a smile.

Mr. Hartley shrugged, obviously in the habit of deflecting these emotions from his beloved. "It matters not, my love, for it has brought me home to England, and in quite the most interesting way. I could not obtain packet passage from Calais. Now that the Peace is upon us, it seems that everyone wants to either come to England or go to France, so I fell into the company of the most interesting chaps—freetraders—"

"FREE—" Emily clutched at her cousin's arm and laid a finger against her own lips, with the result that Miranda remembered to lower her voice to the whispers in which they had all been speaking before. "...traders," she finished rather weakly. "Charles, my love, smugglers?"

"Exactly, my dearest," Mr. Hartley continued dreamily, Miranda's reproofs and his Viennese disgrace quite forgotten. "And by the most fortunate coincidence, they landed their cargoes—spirits and French silk—only a short distance up the coast from the place where my beloved lay sleeping. They were a rather interesting set of chaps, I must say. Why did you know that—"

"No, and I have no wish to, either," Miranda said not quite firmly. The fingers that she put to her lips seemed to be concealing her smile. "Dearest Charles, what next?"

Emily would have liked to hear more of Mr. Hartley's adventures with the famous smugglers of the Sussex coast, but there was such danger in her cousin's demeanor that she deemed it best to hold her peace for the time being.

But Miranda seemed to be calming down. With a resigned sigh, she took Mr. Hartley's hand and gazed long into those blue eyes. "Dear Charles, I am not at all a managing female, I hope, but surely you must see that Sir Francis will never give his consent to our marriage if you do not at least attempt to settle down and direct yourself into more gentlemanly occupations. Perhaps if I were to write to Castlereagh and the Prince, I might be able to smooth things out again—"

Mr. Hartley smiled and shook his head. "I shouldn't, if I were you, my dearest. Anyway, when I was making the Channel with the freetraders—they refer to themselves as the Gentlemen, mind you—I made the most interesting discovery concerning naval navigation—"

Miranda shook her head. "Charles, my love, do you not think it is time to put aside these ridiculous inventions of yours and concentrate upon making a good, gentlemanly career for yourself?"

Mr. Hartley looked a little uncomfortable, but quickly rallied himself to deliver his beloved with one of his devastating smiles. "I mean to put up at the Sanditon Hotel for some time, Miranda, in connection with this project of mine. So, my love, we shall be able to discuss all of this at greater length in the near future." He rose from his chair, seized Miranda's hand and kissed it again, holding it within his own for several seconds.

"Having once again laid eyes upon the life of my heart, I can rest contented," he declared passionately. "And now, I must exit in the same manner in which I made my entrance."

Miranda allowed him to kiss her, and even went so far as to bestow an embrace upon his person. "Dearest Charles, please do try, at least to see the benefit of what I say, for I love you and so much want us to be settled," she sighed in the tones of one addressing a small child. She touched the fringes of his lashes with a sigh. "Go now, before you rouse up the household. All we need is such a scandal!"

With a bow over Emily's hand, Mr. Hartley exited through the window. The cousins watched his descent into the shadows of the moonlight garden.

Emily sighed. "How very much he must love you, Miranda. To be sure, singing songs beneath your window, posting without rest to reach Sanditon...how very nice it must be to be loved like that!"

Miranda yawned. "Yes, I daresay it is all very nice, but not, I assure you, when it interrupts my selfish sleep! My poor Charles! I have a feeling, you know, that I shall spend my married life managing to drag him from one shatterbrained scheme or another." She smiled faintly. "He is the dearest person in the entire world to me, but how much dearer he would be if only he would endeavor to change certain things about his character!"

Emily gave her cousin a sidelong glance, but kept her own silence.

CHAPTER FOUR

Mr. Hartley very properly presented himself at the front door of Number Four, Marine Parade at the hour of ten that next morning. Despite the matter of his having, somewhere, mislaid his card case and his wearing of a cravat which Russet could only consider thoroughly reprehensible for a morning call, Charles was admitted to the presence of the ladies in the morning room.

Russet announced the caller with such subtle disapproval that Lady Rockhall quite frowned him down, but Russet had the last word, for there was a volume of meaning in the manner with which he closed the door behind the hapless Mr. Hartley.

Miranda did not turn a hair as she graciously rose from her chair to greet her swain. "Why, Charles," she said lightly, holding out a hand. "What a surprise to see you here! Whenever did you arrive in England?"

Emily, however, could not quite suppress a deep

blush, and did not know which way to look as her cousin coolly presented Mr. Hartley to Sophia and then to herself. If some small part of that blush was caused by the apprehension that Mr. Hartley was even more handsome in the full light of day than the romantic moonlight of the previous night, she buried these thoughts along with the snail of embroidery she had been picking upon before his entrance and murmured some vague greeting.

Sophia had lived too long in the world to turn a hair at the unexpected arrival of a niece's forbidden beau, and as she bid him to have a chair, and would he take a cup of tea, decided that younger brothers who peremptorily foisted their errant daughters upon her doorstep were only a very few notches above That Woman, for she had also lived too long in the world not to instantly recognize contrivance.

But, Mr. Hartley *did* have lovely eyes, and that fact almost made up for his deplorable lack of the latest gossip from Vienna and his desire to read aloud to the ladies from the manuscript of his latest poem, a rather long and derivative tribute to the full moon rising over the ocean waves. From the rapt attention he was accorded by the two younger females, Sophia decided that poets with fine blue eyes were as much a treat in these sad times as they had been in her youth. Very tactfully, she managed to dissuade him from revising his poem then and there with the stub of a lead pencil he had extracted from a full pocket. Inquiries after certain of her friends then on the Austrian Empire were productive of mutual acquaintance, and only when the conversation veered too closely upon Mr. Hartley's methods of crossing the Channel, or his reasons for his sudden quitting of the Conference did Miranda manage to create diversions, one of which permanently stained

Mr. Hartley's rather sadly rumpled vest with Madeira wine.

"Mr. Hartley invents things, Aunt Sophia," Miranda said a little too brightly as she sponged the rumpled garment with one of her aunt's very best damask napkins. "He's very clever."

Mr. Hartley looked a little startled at this description of himself, but faced with a miniscule dowager in a puce morning dress regarding him with shrewd, rather amused eyes, he could not help but grin with sympathy.

That devastating display of perfect white teeth was another point in his favor, Lady Rockhall decided, and from then on, disregarded the rumpled state of his dress, his habit of suddenly pausing in the middle of a conversation to jot down mysterious scratchings upon his poem-in-progress and his deplorable lack of interest in the affairs and *affaires* of his peers, to devote herself with an awed fascination to waiting for the next eccentricity from this handsome young man. Fatal of course, she decided, but if Miranda must have him, then perhaps some harmless post could be found for him where he would be free to putter about with his poetry and his inventions without too much harm to anyone, and so she would inform that brother of hers when next she saw him.

At the end of a very proper fifteen-minute visit, at Miranda's signal, Charles rose to take his leave. The Dowager gave him her hand and unbent sufficiently to hope that Mr. Hartley would call upon them again very soon, perhaps even come to dinner?

Since this opening allowed Charles to explain his particular theories of cooking and heating with natural gasses, Sophia, who had never in her entire life seen the inside of a kitchen, was again astounded.

Fortunately for her, Admiral Arkwright chose that

57

moment to put in his appearance. Of late, Lady Rockhall's chief *cicisbeo* had been acting more than a little put out by the amount of time and attention his lady had been devoting to her two young charges; time, in his opinion, could be better spent in his company. Catching sight of a disheveled young man of unmistakably poetic aspect ensconced in *his* chair, the Admiral's heavy brows drew together, and he thrust out his lower lip very much like a spoiled child.

"Hartley, hey?" he growled upon being introduced, deliberately and uncomfortably fitting his ample posterior to a fragile, angular chair some distance from the hearth, regarding Mr. Hartley with patent disapproval. "Had one of your cousins under me on the old *Boniface* back in '89 or so. Fellow was a wretched sailor. Always sick. Never knew a Hartley yet to be shipshape and Bristol fashion in the Navy."

Charles had survived Vienna only by his habit of oblivion to the disapproval of older, more organized men, and this sulky thrust passed completely over his head. "I fear sir, that none of my family are particularly nautical—or military either, for that matter. But you speak, I believe of my cousin Robert—" Charles smiled his disarming smile. "I do believe that they—the younger officers, sir, used to refer to you as Old Ironbottom."

Emily gave a stifled gasp. The Dowager's snort may have been a suppressed chuckle, but Miranda was immediately upon her feet, smiling a little stiffly, as she paced the space between the admiral and the poet.

"Aunt, Mr. Hartley has not seen the sights of Sanditon as yet, and I know that you and Admiral Arkwright have much that you wish to discuss—indeed, Emily andI have interrupted your days quite sadly, I fear." She cast a pleading look upon Sophia.

Emily immediately came to her cousin's rescue. "I

quite agree with Miranda, Gran'mama, we have deprived you and Admiral Arkwright of your comfortable coses. Personally, I can think of nothing I would rather do than have a stroll about the town—so much to see, you know, and the sunlight is so particularly lovely this morning—".

"But I've *seen*—" Mr. Hartley protested, only to find Miranda's nails digging into the small of his back. From long experience, he knew that this was her signal to hold his peace, and fell silent, wondering what in the world he had done this time.

"Yes, yes, of course," Sophia said, gesturing them away. "Do you run upstairs and make yourselves ready to walk out, and the three of us shall have a comfortable chat." She waved a hand vaguely in the air at the girls, dismissing them. "Henry, Mr. Hartley was just telling me the most fascinating facts about gas-heating," she said wickedly.

As the girls scurried up the stairs for pelisses and bonnets, Emily repressed a giggle. "Miranda, I do believe she's enjoying this!"

"I'm *not*," Miranda replied sullenly.

Emily was relieved to find her duties as chaperone of this unusual pair were not to be onerous. Miranda was put out with Charles for his gaffe in the morning room, and Mr. Hartley, ready to be pleased by whatever was presented to his sunny attentions, barely noticed his love's sulks, for he found that Emily had the sort of mind that easily grasped the principles of engineering and mechanics, and was quite content to reexpound his theories of natural gas as the trio strolled along the Strand in the bright morning sunlight.

Charles dutifully admired the newest structures of the town, discoursed upon the organic formation of seashells and extolled the benfits of sea bathing, even for the most delicate female constitution. It was only to be

59

expected that he would fall into reveries over the gaslighting at the new Duke's Theatre, and spend a full half hour in earnest conversation with the engineer of this project until Miranda impatiently summoned him away for a visit to the old town and the boatyards.

Skirting the sandy hill which separated the old fishing village from the new Regency resort, he paused only once or twice to admire the view and make addenda to his poem while both ladies sat upon a rock and gazed out across the ocean, one somewhat petulant and squirming to be on, the other wrapped in quiet contemplation of the beauty of the day. Again, Mr. Hartley dutifully admired the quaintness of the old village architecture, and again he became entirely engaged in nautical conversations with the boatbuilders over matters so esoteric that even Emily's patience was tried. Miranda's murmurings were bordering upon the shrewish, and to divert any possible quarrels, at least in her presence, for Emily had a great dislike of harsh words, she gently suggested that perhaps they might all repair to the charming little inn for tea and a luncheon.

This fortunate suggestion diverted both Charles and Miranda, and the impending storm seemed to have abated somewhat by the time they had consumed a pot of tea and some cold beef and bread and finished off their repast with cherry tarts in the dark and charming old hostelry.

With restored spirits, they emerged from the low doorway into the sunlight. "When we are married, Charles," Miranda was saying in the tone one might employ with a small, recalcitrant child, "we shall—"

Mr. Hartley, who had been only vaguely attending to the pronouncements of his ladylove, gave a sudden start and took it upon himself to hail a stalwart, deeply tanned individual striding down the street with a clay pipe clenched firmly in his teeth. "Jem! I say, Jem Hawkes!" Mr. Hartley called, hastening his pace, oblivious to the ladies trailing behind him.

For a split second, the man stiffened in his tracks, and his hand went to the belt at his waist, but upon beholding Mr. Hartley, his rough visage relaxed into a grin.

"It's our Mr. Hartley, the gentleman from Vienna," he said, extending his hand. "I see you made it to Sanditon all right and tight."

Charles nodded affably. "Indeed, indeed I did, and it was an adventure, to be sure."

Mr. Hawkes shook his head and shifted his pipe from one side of his jaw to the other. "'Tisn't the same as it was when we had Boney across the Channel. Freetradin' gets harder all the time, with the riding officers bein' in the neighborhood these days." He shrugged. "Ah, well, no use cryin' over spilt milk, as me missus says."

Charles pushed his hands into his pockets. "You know, Mr. Hawkes, I have been giving some thought to the problem of your compass."

Hawkes raised his brows, interested. "Have you, now?" he asked casually, with all the air of a man who will stand in the street and discuss matters of business for days.

To Miranda, the freetrader looked rather more like a prosperous merchant than a bloodthirsty smuggler. Rather disappointed, she joined Emily upon the bench in the inn courtyard, waiting for the men to finish their conversation. It would never do, she understood, for two young ladies to acknowledge a notorious outlaw, no matter how that outlaw and all his kind were condoned by all levels of Sanditon society.

Emily cast an uneasy glance at her cousin, fully expecting that restless female to exhibit a case of the fidgets. But Miranda was merely studying Mr. Hawkes from beneath the shade of her parasol, her face set in a thoughtful expression which Emily found impossible to gauge.

Being Sussex born and bred, the freetraders were, for her, a fact of life. Even her Papa looked the other way when one of the outbuildings was used to store illicit cargo moving inland, and he was wont to boast that his brandy tasted all the much better for not having been subjected to customs duty, and the very cambric dress she wore had been made up from smuggled material bought cheap by her Mama's woman. Of course, it was not precisely respectable for a gentleman to be seen engaging in open converse with one of the freetraders, but, her kind heart told her, Mr. Hartley was a poet, and as such was above lesser mortals in his choice of companions. One only had to think of Lord Byron to understand *that*.

After some quarter hour's conversation, Mr. Hartley and Mr. Hawkes parted, the freetrader strolling down the street whistling between his teeth.

It did not occur to Mr. Hartley that abandoning his ladies for a conversation with a smuggler was in any way out of the ordinary, and when Miranda rather waspishly pointed this fact out to him, he seemed genuinely puzzled.

"Man's a friend of mine. Presented me with a most unusual problem of navigation and compasses," he explained as they made their way over the hill toward the new town again.

Miranda sighed and shook her head. "The only way you can possibly redeem yourself, Charles, is to escort us to the concert tonight at the Assembly Rooms."

Mr. Hartley shook his head. "Impossible, my dear. I am engaged to meet with Mr. Hawkes and his friends at the Keg and Anchor, an inn up the coast. I shall be providing him with what I believe is called a cover, should the riding officers decide to look too closely at his activities. Mr. Hawkes has a cargo of French silk that he must dispose of, you see."

"Oh, Charles!" Miranda exclaimed. "Do not get involved with these gallows birds! Indeed, your taste for low company sometimes frightens me."

"It is a debt of honor," Mr. Hartley said simply. "They were kind enough to provide me with transport across the Channel, and now I must display my trust in them by repaying my debt. As I say, Miranda, this compass, if it can be tried, could be quite an important thing—"

"Oh, hang the compass, Charles," Miranda said. "Why do men always get to have all the adventures?" She turned her parasol about on her shoulder for a few paces, then laid her hand against his arm. "French silks? I imagine they could be had very cheaply, do you not?" she asked innocently.

"Miranda, you cannot—you will not! I forbid it!" Mr. Hartley said with a great deal of firmness.

"Oh, nonsense," Miranda replied sweetly, tucking her arm into his. "What would make the difference?"

"Miranda," Emily said a little breathlessly, "you would not render Charles for the magistrates for a few yards of silk!"

"Of course not," Miranda replied complacently. "I mean to come with him."

"No," said Mr. Hartley and Miss Rockhall in the same breath.

Miranda thrust out her chin. "I've behaved exactly as Sir Francis would wish for an entire week now, and it's been deadly dull. What harm can there be in going to look at some material? You said yourself, Emily, that everyone deals with the freetraders. In Spain—"

"My dearest Miranda, this is hardly Spain, and as

there are riding officers in the vicinity, I daresay it would not be proper to expose you to the danger—"

Miranda shook her dark curls and smiled.

Whether it was ultimately the boredom of so sedate a round of pleasures, or something deeper and darker lurking in the Brandywine blood which impelled her, she insisted upon accompanying her beau upon the adventure. That everyone in every station of life had dealings with the freetraders was common knowledge. Sophia candidly admitted more than once that her cellars were stocked from the Gentlemen's stores, and if truly pressed, Sanditon's more fashionable modistes would have to tell that their creations were made from untaxed French laces, silks and cambrics. Of course such purchases were made indirectly and discreetly, for it never would have done to alert Inland Revenue's attention to such exalted persons as the residents of Sanditon having dealings with the freetraders. And certainly no lady of Miranda Brandywine's quality would ever have direct dealings with such persons. All of which might have explained why she was determined to purchase a length of French cambric from such unusual sources.

Arguments were raised, very properly, and each one defeated Miranda in the experience of Spain, Vienna or wherever, for to hear her tell the tale, she had been exposed to far worse dangers than could be found upon the Sussex coast. In the end, Charles capitulated; he had seen Miranda deal with equal force with Spanish banditti and the nobility of several nations.

In short shrift, Miss Brandywine prevailed over her cousin's tearful protestations and the vague disapproval of her beau.

At ten o'clock that evening, after assuring herself that the household had retired for the night, Miranda garbed herself in her oldest habit, a still-dashing affair of teal sarcenet trimmed with brass buttons and silk frogs, set a cap upon her head, bade her uneasy cousin a jaunty farewell and climbed out upon the heavy ivy vines that Mr. Hartley had employed to climb upwards upon.

By the time she had reached the garden, Miranda's spirits were slightly dampened, and she was cursing, beneath her breath in a most military fashion, upon the custom which forbade females the wearing of trousers. Disentangling the long train of her habit from the clinging tendrils and brushing ivy leaves out of her hair, she crossed the garden and opened the back gate which led into the mews way.

As promised, Mr. Hartley was awaiting her, mounted upon one hired horse and leading another. Miranda, ruffled from her exit, cast an eye upon the second horse. "Do you really expect me to ride that spavined nag?" she demanded in a hoarse whisper as Charles kissed her cheek and tried to throw her up into the saddle. "Really, my love, you are no judge of horseflesh...."

Mr. Hartley cut short this protest by forcing her into the saddle with some strength. "If you think it's a simple matter to rent a ladies hack for this hour of the night from the hotel, Miranda, I wish you may try it sometime..."

"You should have bribed the ostlers," Miranda said into her collar. "Really, Charles, I always have to think of everything—I hope you did remember—"

He threw back his fine-boned head and eased himself into the saddle. He was not, Miranda noted sadly, a man who appeared to advantage upon a horse, and the look he was delivering her from his fine blue eyes was anything but poetic adoration. "I felt the muse descend upon me, and just as I was about to take up my pen in hand, I recalled my engagement with you." This was pronounced in such accusatory tones that Miranda decided it was best to hold her tongue. Charles, when his poetic muse was in possession of the field, tended to forget all else, including social engagements. It was clear that he was making her a very great sacrifice.

She bit her lip. "Dearest Charles, I am sure that you will forgive me... but a poem can wait, an *adventure* cannot."

Mr. Hartley did not reply, but set his horse to a walk, and none too much in charity with one another, the affianced couple set out for the Keg and Anchor.

The moonlight washed upon the beach, and Miranda, who had been, she felt, cooped up far too long, urged her docile nag into a fair canter through the surf, leaving Charles somewhat behind. The horse at first took exception to the rolling waves, and looked very like it desired to bolt, but Miranda's hands were firm on the reins, and it was not too long before they reached an accord.

She cantered for a half mile before it occurred to her that Charles was not keeping apace. Reluctantly, she reined in and turned to look back down the empty stretch of sand, sighing with impatience.

Mr. Hartley's unpredictable muse had descended upon him again, and he was ambling along at a slow trot, his notebook propped against the saddle, industriously penciling out some lines of verse. It was upon the tip of Miranda's tongue to reprimand him most strongly when she recalled that there was nothing he disliked half so much as being interrupted with his poetry, and so she contented herself with awaiting him, then riding along beside in disdainful silence as he scribbled and murmured to himself. "When in moonlight, I have seen... no, that's not quite it... When in moonlight, I beheld these waves..." Charles murmured, oblivious to Miranda's presence in this most romantic setting.

Miranda, who, if truth were to be told, did not really care for poetry, steeled herself to patience and forbearance—and a gentle trot the five miles which led to the premises of the Keg and Anchor.

Smugglers' dens, Miranda thought with a trace of disappointment, should be dark and sinister places, set high on cliffs above crashing waves, and approached only in storms. The Keg and Anchor, by contrast, seemed that most mundane of erections, a snug little country inn nestled among the pine trees of the forest, looking out upon the peaceful seascape where three small vessels bobbed at their moorings. Geraniums flourished in its window boxes, and calico curtains hung up against the windows, through which cheerful candlelight shone out upon the yard.

There could be no mistaking this rather bucolic setting for anything other than the place of assignation, Miranda noted with a twinge, for a sign representing a keg and an anchor swung to and fro on the ocean breeze.

"Is this the place?" she demanded incredulously, reining in her horse. The ancient nag gave a snort of agreement and hung its head, refusing to move any further.

"What place?" Charles said vaguely, glancing up. "Oh, oh, yes, of course. Yes, my dear, this is the place. The Anchor and Crown."

"Keg and Anchor," Miranda corrected drily, as Charles helped her dismount.

"Quite so, quite so," he murmured, peering into the darkness.

A wholesome looking young ostler emerged from the direction of the stables to take charge of their horses, and Charles and Miranda entered the hallway.

From the snug-looking ordinary, Miranda heard the low sounds of male conversation and smelled the familiar odor of tobacco. Why, she thought, peeling off her gloves, it was no more exciting than an officers' mess, and not half as noisy, nor noisome. Nonetheless, she strained to peer beyond Charles into the room, hoping for some sight of cutthroat desperadoes. If there was illegal trading going on, it was certainly being conducted with a fair amount of discretion.

"Ah, Mr. Hartley." A stout landlady, her starched skirts rustling about her ankles, moved down the passageway toward them.

"How do you do, Mrs. Everley?" Charles asked, as the devoutly respectable-looking female caught sight of Miranda and frowned in such a way that the girl felt a blush rising to her cheeks.

"Ah, this is my sister, Miss Hartley. I, er, had to bring her. Couldn't leave her at the Sanditon Hotel by herself, y'know."

This explanation failed to satisfy the landlady completely, Miranda knew, but she dropped a reluctant curtsey, and observing the cut and style of Miranda's habit as Quality make, relaxed imperceptibly. "Well, then, and I suppose Miss would like the private parlor?"

Miranda was about to protest that she wished to follow Charles into the tap, but he squeezed her arm quite firmly. "Of course, Mrs. Everley. We shall only be a few moments, and I think it's best that she's secured...."

Before Miranda could protest, she was being shepherded down the hallway away from Charles and firmly deposited in a small, oak-paneled chamber where a warming fire cast a soft glow over the old, polished furnishings. Mrs. Everley held the door for her. "I'll send the girl to you as soon as she can be spared," she said firmly, and closed the door on her own muttered "And Mr. Hartley such a *nice* young man!"

Miranda gave an exasperated sigh as a burst of loud

laughter rose from the ordinary. But the fire was warm and inviting in the grate, and she suddenly realized that she was chilled through. With a sulky motion, she tossed her gloves and cap into a chair in a dark corner and turned to sweep her damp skirts before the grate.

"Very handsome accessories, ma'am, but I am not your butler," a deep masculine voice rumbled from the darkness.

Miranda whirled about, her hand diving into the pocket of her habit for the little pistol her father had never allowed her to travel without. In the dancing shadows, she was just able to make out a seated figure wearing a coat of several capes and a pair of gleaming Hessians, proffering her cap and gloves in one hand. Languidly, his shadowed face seemed to smile, and he dangled the items in her direction with a mocking gesture.

None too politely, Miranda snatched back her possessions, regarding the shadowed face with an awareness that the firelight exposed her rising blush to his scrutiny as well as it hid him from her own. "I was not aware that this parlor was occupied, sir," she said stiffly, her hand closing about the mother of pearl butt of the pistol. "You might have had the courtesy to warn me—"

"Before you lifted your skirts to the fire. But then I should have missed a glimpse of a very prettily-formed ankle, and I am not the man to miss my opportunities, you see," he said sardonically, rising to his feet and making her a sweeping exaggerated bow.

"I—I beg your pardon?" Miranda asked in her most frigid accents, tones which had been able to freeze even the most encroaching young officers in Vienna.

But the man only gave a slight toss of his head as he shifted toward the mantelpiece, putting his weight against the broadstone. He was slightly below the ordinary height, Miranda noted, but it did nothing to detract from the muscular set of his shoulders beneath the driving coat, nor the well-curved shape of his legs in buckskin breeches, nor the well-shaped foot which rested negligently against the grate. "It won't do, ma'am, you cannot expect any man to be less than human when suddenly—and so delightfully unexpectedly—presented with such a tiny bit of perfection," he said slowly.

Miranda drew herself up to her full height, still finding herself at the disadvantage of looking up into a pair of darkly amused eyes set beneath thick blond brows. "By the style of your dress, sir, one might imagine you to be a gentleman if your manners did not so obviously indicate the opposite," she sparred warily.

He shook his head, chuckling. A log fell in the grate, and by the rising tongue of flame, she caught his features, rough-hewn and slightly weathered, his curling hair sun-bleached to the color of bronzed gold. His amusement gave his thin lips a sardonic twist in the shadows; there was something of the swashbuckler about him that Miranda found both frightening and attractive.

"Perhaps you are right, ma'am," he agreed, good-humoredly. "I am definitely not a gentleman, as my friends and family are forever reminding me. But then, this is hardly the place where one would expect to find a lady, either."

Miranda's temper flared, and the hand which gripped the tiny pistol moved swiftly out of her pocket as he leaned toward her, only to be caught in a lightning grip, as strong as steel. The blond brows shot up in surprise as he gently squeezed the gun out of her grasp and into the palm of his other hand.

"Here now, the little cat has claws!" he exclaimed, still holding a struggling Miranda at arm's length as he turned the gun over in his hand. "But the next time you go to pull a pistol on a man, make certain that it's cocked, if you please," he said as he handed it back to her, grip first.

Miranda snatched the gun out of his hand, pushing it deep into her pocket, still blushing furiously.

"Shooting an unarmed man who has no designs upon you is hardly sporting, you know," he said in gentler tones, shaking his head. "Whatever is the world coming to when one encounters young Females of Quality in smugglers' inns, armed with poppers?"

Miranda dropped her gaze from his and kicked at the grate with her foot, feeling very foolish, and very much like a child caught out in a prank. "I came to buy some silk," she said sulkily, knowing full well that he had the advantage of her. She was not a lady, she did not belong here, and she felt suddenly foolish and dreadfully embarrassed. "I came with my fiancé to purchase some silk from the freetraders."

"Ah," said the gentleman, as if that explained all. "No doubt, like many another lady who has followed the drum, you find the restrictions of peacetime as confining as the Seraglio?"

Miranda shot him a sharp glance, but the mysterious gentleman's smile was as enigmatic as ever.

Suddenly, there was a shout from the taproom, and the sound of heavy boots upon the wooden floor. Swift as a cat, the gentleman eased toward the door and opened it a crack, his hand reaching inside his coat to remove a businesslike-looking pistol. With a muttered curse, he pushed the gun into his pocket again and closed the door upon the commotion, shaking his head, his eyes suddenly serious, his lips set into a tight line. "It's the riding officers, and they have a warrant," he said tersely to Miranda. "Now, here's the devil, my girl."

For an instant Miranda felt the familiar mingling of fear and excitement, but then recalling that she was in England, not in war-torn Spain, she felt, for the first time in her life, a quavering sense of panic. It was quite one thing to have an adventure, but something else entirely to be brought up before a magistrate, and in such a situation, when she had sworn to be upon her best behavior!

"Charles!" she breathed, and moved toward the door. "He will never be able to explain us out of this— must—" Her hand was upon the brass latch when the gentleman seized her gently, but with a great deal of firmness, by the shoulders and drew her away.

"You little fool! What in hell do you think you're doing? The ordinary's as full as it can hold of soldiers and smugglers, all of them itching for a fight, and whoever you are, I have the certain feeling that you wouldn't relish a night in jail!"

"Charles—my fiancé—out there—arrested or worse!" Miranda gasped, struggling in the man's grip as a shot rang out over the confusion of noise.

"Then your precious Charles is as mad as you, my girl, to drag you both into this rare mess!"

Miranda shook her head impatiently. "You do not understand! Charles would be no use whatsoever in a fight! He has no tactics or strategy—he is a poet!"

"Oh, Lord!" the man muttered with a certain reverence in his exclamation.

"In the name of the King, I place you all under arrest!" someone shouted, and there was the crash of a heavy piece of furniture.

Miranda was as near tears as she had ever been in her life. "Oh, please, let me go!" she pleaded. "It's all my fault, and if they've shot Charles, then I shall surely be routed!"

The man glanced at the door then back at Miranda.

'You're both mad," he remarked matter-of-factly as Miranda winced at the sound of a body slamming into the dividing wall. Quickly, he pushed her into a chair. 'You stay there, do you understand, my girl? If you move as much as a muscle, it will be the worse for you. When I come back, you must agree to whatever I say!"

Too numb to argue, Miranda merely nodded miserably.

The minutes beat past her as agonizing as distant cannons. Gradually, the sound of the scuffle in the ordinary subsided, but strain as she might, she could make nothing of the mutter of men's voices; the ancient, daubed walls of the inn were too thick.

She thought she would scream when the door opened again, and it took all of her badly shaken self-control to remain seated in the chair, her hands folded tightly in her lap, seconds away from the comforting grip of her little pistol. But the face she turned toward the uniformed man carrying a brace of candles was calm enough, and perhaps even a little haughty.

"As you can see, officer, there is only my sister here," the mysterious gentleman was saying smoothly over the soldier's shoulder.

The riding officer, whose insignias gave him the rank of lieutenant, and whose pink cheeks proclaimed he was not long out of his teens, stood in the doorway for a second, staring openmouthed at the young lady who faced him, squaring her shoulders in a manner that reminded him woefully of his major's lady, a most military female.

"Ah, my dear, he's been at it again," the gentleman said as he half dragged, half pushed a very disheveled Charles into the room. Mr. Hartley's cravat was entirely gone, and the seam of his coat sleeves had separated almost entirely from the body of the garment. Worst of all, Miranda spotted the beginnings of a blackened bruise forming about his left eye, and a small trickle of blood running down his chin. He looked rather dazedly at Miranda, as if he could not quite recall who she might be, or the circumstances which surrounded him.

Miranda gave a start, but catching the gentleman's warning glance, forced herself to stay seated in the chair. "So, I see," she said tartly. "He has been at it again. How long will this go on?" she added, taking a risk.

"The gentleman says this is your husband, ma'am?" the young officer asked dubiously. Despite his youth, Miranda noted that his eyes were suspicious.

She nodded briskly. "Indeed that is my husband, although how I came to be married to such a—a *loose fish* is beyond me. Charles, how could you?"

Mr. Hartley blinked at her once or twice and opened his mouth, but the gentleman shifted his weight and took Charles' arm about his own shoulders, half-dragging him further into the room and depositing him carelessly into a chair. "You see, it is as I told you, officer. I do not know how many times m'sister and I have been forced to track him down in some low inn or another, drinking with hedge birds." The gentleman allowed his nostrils to quiver slightly, and he raised a handkerchief to his nose. "A few brandies, and he fancies himself to Great Jackson. Terrible trial on my sister, y'know. It's the full moon," he added in a lower tone of voice. "Runs in the family."

The young officer looked at Mr. Hartley, then at Miranda. "But he was in the company of men known to be freetraders—we may not find anything on this raid, but we'll have our evidence—"

Miranda forced herself to her feet. "That, sir," she announced in strained accents, "is no concern of ours." She knelt over Charles and dabbed at his bloody chin

74

with her handkerchief. "Oh, to think that I should be reduced to this," she said tragically. "To think that the man I married has been driven to madness by that foul, nasty sport of *boxing!*" She looked up at the gentleman. "Before you introduced him to London ways, he was as gentle as a lamb. Now, do you look and see what your raking influence has done, brother dear! And what am I to tell your nieces and nephews when they ask me where their poor Papa is? In jail with a pack of smugglers!" She touched the handkerchief to her own eyes and gave a very good performance of crying. "We were all so happy before you came with your nasty, Corinthian London ways! Boxing and blue ruin and—and opium smoking!"

"Opium smoking," the gentleman said, delivering Miranda a very dangerous look indeed.

"Opium smoking?" The riding officer repeated blankly. He was, Miranda noted, beginning to waver. She pressed her advantage.

"Indeed, I thought—I believed that the seaside air of Sanditon, removed from the influence of low company, would restore his mind, but you see? He has only escaped his attendants—Oh, the scandal! The children and I shall never be able to hold up our heads again!" She was beginning to enjoy this, she decided, and might have elaborated even farther had not the mysterious gentleman intervened.

"You see how it is," he murmured to the officer. From his wallet, he extracted a note. "Since there's really no harm done, and no contraband goods on these premises, perhaps you and your men could be persuaded to overlook my brother-in-law's show of temper. When he's in his cups, he does tend to get carried away, you know. Sad trial on the family..." The crisp note rustled in his hand. "You might wish to drink to the possibility of his recovering his health...."

"It ain't drink what brought him low," the young officer said. "He don't smell of no liquor."

"The opium, my good man, the opium," the gentleman said smoothly. "Pray let us not have to drag this matter any further. It could cause a great deal of embarrassement...FitzClarence and all that...."

"Planted him a facer, Randa," Charles said deliriously.

"FitzClarence?" The young officer said, rubbing his beardless chin. A heavy sergeant appeared in the doorway.

"We searched the whole house from attic to cellar, sir, and there ain't nothing here that ain't been dutied," he said heavily, in the voice of one who could have told you so before the event.

The young lieutenant flushed. "I see," he said regretfully.

"And exceptin' for this gentleman here a'layin' his fives on Beresford, they ain't naught breakin' of the law," the sergeant added gloomily.

The mysterious gentleman smiled and tactfully fingered the note between his fingers. The lieutenant wavered for a second, then turned. "I guess there's no harm done," he admitted at last, a great deal of grief in his tone. "But in future, sir, I advise you to keep your brother-in-law safely confined."

Stiffly, he turned on his heel and marched down the passageway. The sergeant lingered in the door for a second. The mysterious gentleman smiled, and with a broad wink, the note was transferred from one hand to the other.

"Iffen I were you, sir, I'd have a care as to how I bought my brandy in the future," the sergeant advised, pushing up his hat with a heavy thumb. "Times are getting rougher for these lads and no mistake."

"I shall keep that in mind," the mysterious gentleman replied gravely, and with another wink, the sergeant strode on down the passageway behind his lieutenant.

"Well!" Miranda said with a great deal of satisfaction. "We pulled that off admirably, did we not?"

"You, ma'am, ought to have a horsewhip taken to you," the gentleman replied, bending over Mr. Hartley. "But it was a smashing blow," he added, examining Charles' eye.

Charles managed a smile. "I landed it quite well, I thought. Of couse, I am no pugilist, I am a peaceable man, but I do object to some young johnny raw in a uniform pushing me about!"

The gentleman shook his head, standing up. "I surmise it'll be the last time that young fool tries to bully someone. Tell the truth, I wouldn't have thought you had it in you, sir!"

"Nor I!" Charles admitted, rubbing his jaw ruefully. He shook his head. "Lord, what a foul night this has been!"

"I thought it capital!" Miranda put in.

"And I shall repeat that you ought to be horsewhiped for this night's work," the gentleman said.

"And you, sir, got no better than what you deserved for bringing her along! Take my advice lad and break her to bridle immediately, or she will make your married life a merry hell!"

Miranda started to say something, but was suppressed as the gentleman assisted Charles to his feet. "Do you feel well enough to ride?"

"I believe I can make it. It's but a short distance," Mr. Hartley replied. "But I am in your debt, sir."

"Think nothing of it. In future, however, you would do me a favor if you would keep your fiancée safely at home when I venture out to stock my brandy!"

* * *

The clock on the landing had chimed four, and Emily's candle was guttering in its socket when she heard the scraping at the windowsill. Almost hysterical with her own vivid imagination, she assisted her cousin to drag herself and her bedraggled skirts over the sill.

"Are you all right? Is Mr. Hartley all right?" She inquired frantically, her hands brushing at the dirt and ivy which entangled Miranda's person.

Miranda gave a shaky imitation of her own laugh. "In heaven's name, Emily, don't wake the dead! I shall have enough trouble explaining this habit to Maria tomorrow! We only had a bit of an adventure, that's all, and Charles acted very stupidly, and if it were not for the most amazing gentleman, we might be in jail right now!"

Seeing Emily's horrified expression, Miranda patted her cousin's cheek. As she stripped and washed, she recounted the night's adventures to the accompaniment of her cousin's little exclamations of dismay and terror.

"And I daresay, if not for that man, heaven only knows what scandal would have been thrust upon Aunt Sophia! What a very enterprising gentleman he was, to be sure, even though he said I ought to be horsewhiped, and I could really not disagree with him on that point, I fear, because it was a harebrained scheme!" she finished, brushing out her hair before the mirror. Slowly, she turned and looked at Emily, seated upon the edge of the bed, as pale as her nightdress. "Emily, I promise I won't do it again!"

Emily shook her head, folding her arms across her chest. "Poor Mr. Hartley—a blackened eye and a cut lip!" She sighed. "I do hope that he shall be allright—all alone in that hotel, with no one to nurse him—"

"Oh, Charles will survive, I assure you," Miranda replied drily.

"But, Miranda, how could you—"

The smaller cousin sat down and put her arm about Emily's shoulders. "You were quite right to worry, Emily, and I was quite, quite wrong to become involved in such a shatterbrained adventure, and I hope you will not waste your time worrying over 'poor Charles' because, my love, I assure you that he will be just fine. It is only when I think of what dreadful scandal might have befallen poor Aunt, and how awful it would all look that I seriously feel queasy! I will not do it again, I promise!"

With those words, Emily had to be comforted.

But she could not help but feel even more uneasy. Miranda on her best behavior was likely to be far more worrisome than Miranda embarked upon an adventure.

CHAPTER FIVE

It might have been expected that a lady who has, within the space of a night, encountered smugglers, a mysterious gentleman and a narrow escape from a scandalous arrest would find herself inclined to lie abed until the next afternoon, but Miranda appeared in the morning room at ten, looking none the worse for her adventure.

On the contrary, it was Emily whose pale face and shadowed eyes betrayed signs of exhaustion, and Miss Rockhall who winced and declined when Miranda suggested a morning sea bathe might be just the thing.

It was determined that the ladies would spend a quiet morning at home, and by the time Lady Rockhall had been released from two capable hands of her dresser, she found both her young charges occupied with their correspondences in the sunlight of the morning room.

"What, no callers?" my lady asked bracingly as she entered the room, trailing her own mail in her wake.

"I fear we have sadly declined in popularity," Miranda said gaily as she sealed a letter to her father with a drop of wax. "Indeed, it looks as if we shall have a very quiet day—"

Russet chose that moment to enter the room. Although his face was the impassive mask of the perfect servant, a slight twitch above one eyebrow betrayed a certain angst to Sophia.

"Lord Marle is arrived, my lady," he said in slightly apprehensive tones. "I took the liberty of placing him in the Green Salon."

He could not have produced a more calculated reaction if he had announced that Armageddon was taking place upon the Strand. Miranda froze above her letter, her eyebrows rising toward her dark curls in surprise. Sophia, momentarily stricken in her efforts to place Lord Marle, merely looked blank. But Emily, whose worst nightmares had been suddenly realized, gave a small shriek, and started up from her chair, her eyes as round as saucers, one hand pressed against her breast, her pale face suddenly almost skeletal, her lips opening and closing soundlessly.

"Oh, Lord," Miranda said succinctly.

"Marle," Sophia said in tones of comprehensive memory. Her jaw dropped. "Oh, *Marle!*" she repeated in sudden understanding.

"Lord...Marle..." Emily whispered, wringing her hands. She sank back into the chair, staring blankly at Russet's immobile face.

How much longer this tableau might have lasted had not Miranda snapped to her senses remained a matter of interesting speculation to Russet, for that lady suddenly rose from her chair and crossed the room to her cousin, laying her hand firmly about the trembling shoulder.

Sophia, having recalled precisely who Lord Marle

81

was, and why she did not wish to have him pay a morning call, made a commendable effort to pull herself together. Every inch the grand dowager, she nodded regally toward Russet. "Thank you. We shall join him there directly," she said, clasping her hands before her, giving Russet a gesture of dismissal.

With one of his long, meaningful looks at his employer, the butler retired belowstairs to regale the hall with the stirrings of rare drama that were about to transpire above.

"Emily," Miranda said as soon as the door had closed upon the butler, "you must pull yourself together."

"The letter, Miranda, you said that if he received the letter, he would not—"

"What letter?" Sophia asked, all at sea.

"Emily, this is not the time for Cheltenham tragedy," Miranda said dangerously.

"No, it is not," the Dowager added thoughtfully. "He must be received."

"We are here," Miranda reminded her, "and no matter how you feel about Lord Marle, it behooves you to greet him civilly."

Emily shook her head violently, clutching at her grandmother's arm. "Please, do not let him carry me away!" she pleaded.

"Of course not!" Sophia replied. "A very strange thing it would be, if we were to allow someone to carry you off in broad daylight on the Marine Parade. It would look very odd to the neighbors, I'm sure."

"You must see him, Emily," Miranda said. "It will only take a little firmness, you know."

"I shall certainly not allow that odious man to bully my granddaughter in my house, no matter what That Woman may allow in her domicile," Sophia added. "Indeed, if he is in the least encroaching, I shall deliver im a strong setdown. A very strong setdown," she muttered to herself.

"Oh, pray!" Miss Rockhall pleaded in a small voice, looking desperately from her cousin to her grandmother, "do not abandon me to be all alone with him!"

"Certainly not!" Miranda agreed bracingly. "Aunt and I shall be with you the entire while. Whatever he has to say, he may say to all three of us!"

"Quite so," the Dowager nodded. "Now, my love, do try and pull yourself together—you look a fright, and nothing, rest assured, will put a female to disadvantage more than looking a fright. We shall see about Marle!" There was a certain light in her eye which suggested that she was not at all adverse to confronting the man who had thrown her beloved granddaughter into such a dreadful fright of nerves.

Even with such forceful allies, it took several minutes to persuade the cowering Emily to put her hair aright and straighten her gown. Miranda, whose patience was not long, was sorely tried by her cousin's timidity, but Lady Rockhall exercised a great deal of tact and soothing words to bring the girl around. When she was perfectly satisfied that Emily would not bolt from the room or collapse into a fit of hysterics, her grandmother took her hand, and with Miranda guarding her other flank, Emily was able to make the journey from the morning room to the salon.

The gentleman seated in the Green Salon pursuing an ancient issue of *Le Belle Assemblée* had his back toward the door, but this was fortunate, for he did not witness Emily's attempt to escape from her cousin and grandmother. But as Miranda was stroking her cousin's hand, she frowned at the golden head bent over the pages, sensing something uncomfortably familiar about the set of those shoulders.

"Good day, Lord Marle," Emily said in a high clear

83

voice only slightly tinged with nerves, and his lordship turned and rose to his feet.

To be confronted with the sight of one's betrothed flanked on one side by a formidable dowager in a purple turban and an equally intimidating cousin staring down the Brandywine nose upon the other was not a sight most affianced men would care to face, particularly since both guards seemed, upon first impression, to be determined to kill with the coldness of twin medusa stares. But Lord Marle was not like most affianced men, and as he moved forward to make his bows, he had the advantage of seeing the cousin's face pass through a most entertaining series of expressions.

For Lord Marle was none other than Miranda's mysterious rescuer of the previous evening!

Miranda heard the introductions being made from a great distance away; she was aware of a faint scarlet blush stealing up the neckline of her ivory morning dress, and aware that Lord Marle was bowing over her hand with the faintest trace of a roguish glint in his eye. "Miss Brandywine," he said smoothly, and how very well she knew that smoothness of tone.

"My lord," she heard herself replying, automatically kicking back the deep hems of her skirts for a slight curtsey.

"I do believe I have had the pleasure of your acquaintance elsewhere," Lord Marle was saying.

"For the life of me, I do believe you are familiar," Miranda replied. "But I cannot quite place—" The thought that he might betray her crossed her mind and she shot him a sharp look.

But he merely nodded, as if unable to recollect, and took the chair which Lady Rockhall indicated to him.

Seating herself and gesturing Emily into the couch beside her, Sophia frankly appraised Lord Marle. It was clear that she was trying to recall exactly what injustices he had done her granddaughter, and equally clear that she was slightly disappointed that he was not an ogre.

In fact, Miranda observed as she uneasily seated herself between the viscount and Emily, Lord Marle was rather a handsome man when seen in the sunny daylight of her aunt's parlor. This morning he was very correctly attired in a coat of Bath superfine and a set of breeches that needed no padding from his tailor. His waistcoat was a delicate shade of sky blue that set off the single fob upon his watch chain, and his black leather shoes were only ornamented with the plainest of gold buckles, yet altogether, he presented the air of a man of taste, fashion and the wealth to indulge himself. But was this Emily's Nemesis?

"What brings you to Sanditon, Lord Marle?" she baited him, her hands folded in her lap, her ankles daintily crossed beneath her gown.

"I have come to do some business. The buying of horsewhips," he replied without missing a beat. "And of course, to see my fiancée," he added, giving Emily the slightest nod. "I had a letter from Lady Rockhall, telling me that you were in Sanditon, and that I should pay a call upon you," he told Emily.

"She did?" Emily gulped. "T-that is—you did. But I—we—thought you were cruising the coast of Ireland, or France—"

"In my ketch," Lord Marle finished.

Miranda threw him a sharp look from beneath the fringe of her lashes. He's not abrupt, she thought suddenly, he's *bored!* Emily *bores* him! But then, why did he offer for her in the first place?

"...do put into port sometimes, Miss Rockhall," he was saying patiently. "But since I had not heard from you, and I had this letter from your mother, I thought it wise to call upon you."

Emily cast a despairing look at Miranda; it was all too clear that the fatal letter had somehow never managed to catch up with its traveling recipient.

There was an awkward silence as this unhappy fact sunk in between Emily and Miranda. Miss Brandywine, still smarting under Lord Marle's non-too-subtle remark about *horsewhips*, pulled herself together and signaled Emily to remain calm.

But Lord Marle was regarding his fiancée with a trace of expectancy. "Your mother, as I have said, asked me to call upon you. I hope that I have not chosen an inconvenient time?"

"Oh, no, that is—" Emily broke off, cowed by the slight impatient edge in his voice. She looked down at the toes of her slippers, just peeking out of the hem of her sprig muslin dress, then desperately, at Miranda. Lord Marle, raising one eyebrow slightly, followed her gaze. Miranda returned the look with a calm expression.

"Your mother seems rather anxious that we should set a date, Miss Rockhall. She feels that there are many preparations to be made." He threw one well-trewed leg across the other, clearly bored with this duty call. "And I had, of course, hoped that you would care to inspect the *Seawind* while she is moored in Sanditon. Since we shall be honeymooning upon her, I wished you to ascertain that all is satisfactorily arranged for your convenience."

"But, Lord Marle, I thought that we—that Mama had arranged that with you. You know that I become terribly seasick—" she quavered.

The viscount shrugged. "Everyone is seasick at times, even me. It is merely a question of getting your legs, as I told you before," he said firmly. "I am certain that Miss Brandywine will tell you that it takes a few days to adjust to the pitch and roll of a boat."

Miss Brandywine, alert for further barbs, merely delivered herself of a speaking look in Marle's direction. "I am sure that you do not mean to tease my cousin about setting a wedding date when it is clear that she is still fagged to death from the rigors of her London Season," she said repressively.

Lord Marle regarded her as if he had not given this point too much consideration, and did not believe that anyone else should either. "That may be all very well, but she has had two weeks rest here in Sanditon, and I am anxious that she should become accustomed to her duties as mistress of Runford Place and the future Countess Runford as soon as possible. My father, as you must know, Miss Rockhall, is not a well man, and would rest easier if he knew we were buckled at last."

Thinking of that haughty and rather terrifying gentleman ensconced in his great chair, his leg propped up before him upon a gout stool, inspecting her as if she were a slab of meat, Emily shivered.

"Poor Mad Jack!" Sophia said unexpectedly. "Has it come to that, then?"

The viscount permittted himself a thin smile. "Perhaps the same activities which led to m'father's soubriquet of Mad Jack have also led to his illness, ma'am," he replied thinly.

"Fancy that," said the Dowager. "Mad Jack sticking his spoon in the wall after all these years."

"That is why I am most anxious to set the wedding date, ma'am. I am three and thirty and must be thinking of my own heir."

"Your mother was a Trevanion," Sophia replied, apropos of nothing. "I recall her quite well. She was a great beauty in her day, and possessed of a quite extraordinary diamond—a huge thing, it was, and quite imposing."

"The Star of Runford. Yes. When Miss Rockhall becomes my wife, she will wear it."

Emily looked as if she would rather wear a ball and chain, but she managed to produce a sick little smile.

Being obliged to sit through a ten-minute recital of the various eccentrics and loose fish which graced his family tree in the Dowager's youth, Lord Marle did his best to control the smile which rose unbidden to his lips upon this unexpectedly encountering the lady of the French silk adventure as the cousin of his complaisant fiancée. The two cousins were a sharp contrast—it was difficult to imagine the same bloodline had produced both his shy, biddable fiancée and her exasperating, hoydenish cousin. But then it was also quite impossible to imagine Miss Rockhall participating in such a merry scene as Miss Brandywine had led him through the previous night. It was a pleasure to discover that his fiancée's Sanditon relations were by no means as toadeater and obsequious as her parents. Perhaps this dull duty visit to Sanditon would be more exciting than he had originally anticipated.

Having been brought up in full awareness of his station in life as the heir to an ancient earldom and the possessor of a truly magnificent fortune, Marle was well aware of his own arrogance. As he had blithely informed Miranda, even his own family thought his manners were upon the point of rudeness, and his cynicism allowed him to view the fortunate accident of his birth and their effects upon the reactions of others with a certain world-weary amusement. But he had never before had the experience of a small, worldly dowager analyzing the strange fits and starts of his character and reputation against Brandywine Blood. It was evidently a very precious commodity this Brandywine Blood, for the Dowager was subtly letting him know that she held the reins of matriarchal power and entertained Doubts about the intended match. Lady Rockhall put him so strongly in mind of his own grandmother that he was not at all surprised to discover that these two ladies had been rival Georgian beauties.

As soon as was proper, the viscount rose and bowed to the ladies, taking his leave. Seeing that he was not to be granted the opportunity of a private interview with his affianced, and ascribing this state of affairs to her grandmother's Doubts, Marle was content, for the time being, to allow matters to lie where they were. But he could not resist the impulse to linger over Miss Brandywine's hand just a shade longer than necessary, and to meet her innocent-seeming eyes with a glance so frought with meaning that she was forced to bite her lip rather than laugh.

After the door had closed upon his well-tailored form, Emily sank back into her chair, trembling all over, the shredded remains of her handkerchief falling from her lifeless hands to the carpet. Miranda could no longer hide her mirth. "Silly, silly goose!" she chided her cousin. "He's no more a monster than my Charles!"

Fortunately for Miss Brandywine's limited tact, the Dowager chose that moment to inquire about the letter again, and between bursts of laughter, Miranda was obliged to explain it all to her patient aunt, while Emily pulled the fringes of her Norwich shawl between her fingers, looking as if she wished she were a thousand miles away.

To her credit, Sophia digested this bit of information without censoring her granddaughter or her niece upon their impetuous conduct. Instead, she put one finger against her cheek and thought for a minute, regarding them both with her dark eyes.

"For my part, I can see why you, Emily, hold a man like Marle in the greatest apprehension. Those dreadful Runford manners, so very arrogant and incivil, so exactly like his father! But there is a great deal of difference between arrogant manners and cruelty, my love, and I do not think Marle is a cruel man at all."

Emily looked at her grandmother from the eyes of a trapped animal. Her nerves, already wracked by lack of sleep, were now at the breaking point. With a small cry, she rose from her chair, trailing shreds of handkerchief and fringes of her shawl, and ran out of the room.

Miranda and Sophia exchanged glances, and the Dowager pressed her fingers delicately against her forehead. "Modern manners," she said in a strained voice, "are not at all what they should be. In my day, a female took the match her parents made for her, and was glad to have a husband. It is all the influence of That Woman."

Fortunately for Miranda, Admiral Arkwright chose that moment to put in his daily appearance, and she was able to escape to her cousin's chamber.

Emily had flung herself across the bed, where she was staring at the rosy challis of her bed curtains with unseeing, tear-stained eyes.

"Go away!" she said to Miranda without looking at her.

Miranda smiled, disobeying her cousin's order as she closed the door behind her. "That is all you need to say to Lord Marle, and I assure you, he will put his yacht out to sea instantly," she said, seating herself on the edge of the bed. "Emily, listen to me, what I have to tell you is most important!"

"I'm listening," Emily replied in a tone indicating that she was not, at all.

"Lord Marle is the mysterious gentleman!"

Miss Rockhall seized upon this piece of information. Her eyes grew large and she raised her head, betraying interest despite herself.

"Miranda, no!" Emily protested, but Miranda was nodding her head and pressing a hand over her lips in such a way that Emily knew this was not one of her cousin's jests. She sat up even farther, clearly at a loss. "L-Lord Marle was the man who rescued you? But how could the pair of you sit there and speak to one another as if nothing had ever happened?"

Miranda leaned against the bedpost. "Indeed? When he made that remark about horsewhips I thought the game was over! I never wanted to laugh so much in my entire life, and there has never been a situation where it was more imperative that I did *not* laugh! Emily, I wanted to die!" Since she was wreathed in smiles, it was quite clear to her proper cousin that she was not regarding this episode in the right light, at all.

"Miranda," Emily said severely, but Miss Brandywine only shook her head.

"I think he's not quite such a monster, Emily, but he is odiously arrogant, and needs to be taken down a peg or two in his own estimation!"

"Much good that does me," Emily said rather sullenly.

Miranda patted her cousin's hand. "You, my dear, are the only female I know who looks even more beautiful in tears! It will not do for you to cry in front of Marle if you wish to break your engagement."

"Oh, Miranda, it was all I could do not to burst into a shriek when I saw him, and the look he gave me—I should be stone at this moment!"

"No, no, my love, you must not marry him, he is patently the wrong man for you, but I see now why you are afraid to face him, he would not take it at all in a gentlemanly way—I'll wager you anything that he is not the sort who has been used to *any* sort of denial!"

Emily nodded, watching warily as her cousin's face

took on that expression that boded ill for peace-loving folk. "Miranda, you—" she began uncertainly.

"I was just thinking that he is probably not the sort who would wish to marry into a family that holds *me!*" Miranda chuckled. "Horsewhiped! Well, there you have it, my love!"

Emily shook her head. "Lord Marle is very proud. He would never break an engagement."

"Then you must break it yourself!"

Emily looked as if this prospect were even bleaker than a lifetime spent with Lord Marle. "Oh, I could not—Mama would—" she whispered.

"Then we shall have to convince him that it is his idea and that you will not suit!" Miranda plunged on breathlessly. "And the way to do that is to—to—use diversionary tactics!"

"Diversion—I do not properly understand you, Miranda," Emily said suspiciously.

"All is fair in love and war—and this is war!" Miranda declared. "You shall behave in such a manner as to give Marle a disgust of your character. He thinks he must marry to provide a suitable hostess for Runford Place—and to have an heir. It's quite obvious that he has chosen a miss out of the schoolroom because no other female meets his standards! Don't you see, Emily, he wants you because he thinks you can be molded into whatever he wants, that you will be a complaisant wife who will be so grateful for the title and the fortune that she will gladly overlook his personal faults, of which I would name arrogance as the prime one, and probably a slew of mistresses stashed everywhere!"

"Mama said that I was not to mind Mrs. Secombe," Emily sighed. "Mama says that all men keep—mistresses, and that no lady notices such things."

"That sounds very like what your Mama would say," Miranda replied frankly. "But it don't signify, Emily!

92

What we must do is be certain that Marle never has a chance to see you alone—either I shall be with you, or Aunt Sophia, or Charles—" Miranda bit her lip thoughtfully. "Charles. Of course. Emily, do you like Charles?"

"Of course I like Mr. Hartley! He is—he is very kind, and very sensitive!" Emily responded.

Miranda smiled. "That is wonderful above all things, because you and Charles are going to be spending a great deal of time in one another's company, and I shall constantly be placing myself in Marle's path. That way, you see, there is not only no possible way he can seek a private word with you, but also, he will believe that your heart is pledged to another, and that you are a shocking flirt, and besides, with a cousin like me, there could be no possible way that Marle would wish to marry into our family!"

"Me? A shocking flirt?" Emily asked, much astounded.

Miranda patted her hand in a reassuring manner. "Of course. Well, to him, it will look as if you are a shocking flirt, but we shall know you are not."

"But what about Charles—Mr. Hartley? I am sure that his principles would never allow him to agree to such a scheme!"

"Perhaps it would be better if Charles did not know his part," Miranda agreed thoughtfully, biting the tip of her finger. "For whenever we did theatricals, Charles was always a terrible actor. No, I think for the time being, we shall leave him in the dark; he will play his role in a much better fashion if he is ignorant of our true motives! Oh, how thankful I am that I encountered Marle last night!"

"Miranda, I think it is a most shatterbrained scheme," Emily said doubtfully.

But Miranda, once started, was not to be stopped.

"He will only be here for a few days—you heard him say so. So, we only need carry on the deception for a few days. Not even your Mama could possibly blame you if Lord Marle was so ungentlemanly as to break off your engagement, Emily. Now, do you but play your part—which is really no part at all, except to stay out of Marle's path, and I promise you, he will cry off within a fortnight."

"And if he doesn't?" Emily asked.

"Then I shall have to marry him myself, simply to keep you from his clutches!" Miranda laughed.

"What will Charles say? Don't you think that he will be hurt if you conduct yourself so outrageously as you propose?"

Miranda tossed her head. "Oh, Charles is quite used to any fit I take into my head! When I explain it all to him, later, he will be quite the first to see the jest."

Emily merely looked doubtful still, but Miranda, caught in her own tangles, continued blithely on.

CHAPTER SIX

A childhood spent following the drum through a series of garrison towns and dusty Spanish villages under the tutelage of a string of governesses and colonel's ladies had taught Miranda Brandywine to slaughter and dress a chicken with the same aplomb that enabled her to dance through a single pair of slippers in an evening's revels. By the time she put up her hair and let down her skirts, the general's daughter was a veteran campaigner, adept at the ruthless, if completely altruistic, management of lives with the military stratagems of her father. What would work in the battlefield would work in the ballroom, but Miranda had yet to learn that arranging the hearts and minds of those she loved required more than tactics. And that simple little blindness would prove as dangerous as any of Napoleon's cannoneers.

Having made up her mind that Emily, gently nurtured to womanhood in the peaceful isolation of England, stood in desperate need of her help, Miranda was determined to provide it, whether or not Emily truly desired it, and without reflection upon the way in which it would set all their lives at sixes and sevens. Miranda had learned her military lessons all too well. But her heart was large, and her intentions loving.

Anxious to foray into battle, she was slightly disappointed when Lord Marle presented no immediate opportunities for attack.

It came, as attacks often do, several days after she had laid her strategy, and was completely off her guard, seated in the tea pavilion with Mr. Hartley and her cousin after a rather desultory stroll along the shoreline. Emily had managed, with the agile assistance of Mr. Hartley, to acquire a collection of seashells from the crags and boulders along the tideline of the beach, and these she had spread out upon the tea table like the pieces of a board game, with the intention of gluing them to an enameled box in suitable marine patterns, such as those she had seen offered for sale in the Sanditon shops.

With the arrival of his tea and crème rusks, Mr. Hartley's muse had decided to put in an appearance, and at that moment he was lining out words to a seashell in his notebook, respectfully encouraged by Miss Rockhall's admiring attitudes and watchful silence.

Emily refused to enter into any speculations upon the nature and states of the other customers of the pavilion in deference to Charles' muse, and Charles, Miranda knew from experience, could not be budged from his creative labors when inspiration had seized upon him and possessed him to lick the nib on his pencil in a most annoying way while composing. Miss Brandywine had allowed her attention to wander about the pavilion, her speculative gaze hidden modestly beneath the frame of her cottage bonnet, one gloved hand supporting her chin, the listless gloved fingers tangling carelessly in the knot of pink ribands the only betrayal of her boredom.

The day was warm and humid, but an ocean breeze alleviated discomfort even as it ruffled through the flowers upon the ladies' bonnets and disarrayed the careful, careless curls of the gentlemen's coiffures. In the slanting, muted yellowness of the afternoon sunlight, their promenade costumes, although surely of the latest London mode, seemed dowdy and dull and English to her mind, and though these summer residents of Sanditon might placidly congratulate themselves upon being in the fashionable vanguard of sea climes and ocean breezes, she found her own attention slipping toward the distant horizon, where two ketches under mainsail and genoa were riding the blue division between sky and sea.

Quite unexpectedly, and with a certain sense of annoyance, Miranda felt her heart turning in her breast at the unexpected sight of Lord Marle framed by the yellow sunlight in the portals of the pavilion, every inch the fashionable gentleman upon promenade in his well-tailored coat of corbeau broadcloth and his polished Hessians with buff toppings, a walking stick tucked casually beneath one arm, the other hand raising elegantly to place his quizzing glass in his eye as he surveyed the gathering. When his hideously enlarged eye fell upon Miranda's party, she was startled to note that his expression was one of resigned boredom. The glass dropped upon its riband before she had time to settle her own feature into an expression equally offending, and he had turned to admit his companions to the room.

As Miranda beheld none other than Lady Denham, the ancient Sanditon patroness upon whose goodwill any aspirant to *ton* must depend, as Lady Rockhall had fretfully pointed out to her charges, her eyebrows rose slightly. Since the wasp-tongued dowager rarely appeared outside the ancient confines of Denham Place, Miss Brandywine was startled that such a high stickler would make her entrance into the pavilion on the arm of so dubious an individual as Lord Marle. Trailed by a lackluster female companion of indeterminate age, bearing a pair of small dogs of equal status, Lady Denham paused for a second in the portals while Marle bent to whisper something into the ear barely concealed beneath a purple silk turban. Her shrewd eyes fell upon Miranda's table, and with her plumes set full sail, she made her regal procession across the floor, her Malacca cane genteelly acknowledging her acquaintance among those present in the room with a series of small thrusts. She was leaning upon Marle's arm in a manner that Miss Brandywine found positively and very uncharacteristically girlish; so fascinated was she with this scene that she barely had time to give her cousin's sleeve a warning tug before they must all need rise to greet the doyenne of Sanditon.

In the general flurry of introductions, curtseys, bows, acknowledgments of previous acquaintances and polite inquiries, Miranda experienced a moment of anxiety when Charles, in his absentminded way, started to recall the precise circumstances of his previous meeting with Lord Marle. Miranda seeking to cut short these uncomfortable recollections with one well-placed nudge of a pink satin slipper beneath the table found her unintentional target in the solicitous maître d' who was rushing, together with a small army of waiters, to place extra chairs and covers for so influential a guest. Fortunately Charles' most improper story was aborted by the maître d's reaction and the resultant excitement of Lady Denham's nervous pugs. By the time her ladyship had commandeered a chair between Emily and

Miranda, commanded a waiter to remove her two "dear little doggies" for a walk, imperiously commanded the companion, a Miss Denham, to stop whimpering and take that seat beside that handsome young man—was he a Hampshire Hartley? Yes, good—thrust Lord Marle into the seat opposite Miss Brandywine with the tip of her cane and ordered tea and blueberry tarts all around, blueberry tarts being inducive to proper physicking after sea bathing, Mr. Hartley's introduction to recollection was all but forgotten. Miranda, believing them all temporarily relieved of any further discomfort, was about to breathe a sigh of relief when the purple plumes were suddenly turned in her direction, and the silver tip of the cane was pointed in the direction of her bodice.

"Aha! So you're my godson's fiancée," the Dowager said to her without preamble. "Naughty puss, not to bring it to my attention at the Assembly! No need for such false modesty, even if you are the shy puss that Marle says you are! Should have told me—would have invited you to the Place for tea, or whatnot."

Emily blushed as pink as her bonnet strings and turned her head away, but Miranda, who had spent a lifetime dealing with terrifying diplomat's ladies in purple turbans, managed a thin smile, and a slightly lifted eyebrow that conveyed she would rather be dead than married to Marle. "On the contrary, ma'am, it is my cousin, Miss Rockhall, who is at present affianced to Lord Marle," she replied, hoping that Marle had caught the none-too-subtle implications of her words.

Lady Denham, not in the least discomfited, merely gave her a very shrewd look and a nod.

"My fiancé is Mr. Hartley. I am Miranda Brandywine," she said.

"So you're Francis Brandywine's gel? Can't hold a candle to your poor Mama—she was a great beauty, but I daresay you're pretty enough, and from what Vincent has told me, quite an original. Look at me! I was mercilessly plain, I'll have you know, but I managed to snare two husbands with Originality. Be an Original, my gel, and you won't grow wrong!" There was the faintest trace of humor in the Dowager's powdered face as she spoke, and Miranda was almost certain that her ladyship had *winked* at her before turning toward Emily with a barrage of compliments upon her English beauty and a great many questions about her background and style.

Miranda sat silent for a second, staring into the steep depths of her lukewarm tea, at a loss to comprehend this unexpected warmth from a woman not noted for her approval of spirited females.

Across the table, Miss Denham was exclaiming on her admiration of poets, especially the very naughty Lord Byron, a situation which allowed Mr. Hartley the rare purchase of approval. He opened his collar a little further and rewarded the homely spinster with one of his most charming smiles, causing her to coo with maternal delight.

Taken in ambush, outflanked and outmanned on every side, Miranda was torn between the annoyance of being deprived of the first blood in battle, and the very ironic sense of the absurdity of her present situation. She did not know whether to sulk or laugh.

Lord Marle made the choice for her.

"Well, Miss Brandywine, we are ill-met again," he said in a low voice without a trace of malice, as if he had been reading her thoughts. His surprisingly workmanlike hands, as if unused to idleness, moved across the table and selected one of Emily's shells, a delicate pink conch.

Laughter won, but just barely, and Miranda's lips curved upwards, despite herself. "You are quite correct in that, at least. We do seem to encounter one another in the most unusual circumstances, sir."

"And with the most unlikely people."

Miranda nodded. Almost lazily, she selected another shell, a blue-veined fan scallop. "It would almost be on the tip of my tongue to say that we cannot continue to meet like this, if it did not sound so absurdly like something from the lips of some insipid heroine in a novel with a highly moral ending."

Marle put the shell down on the table between them and selected another. "And, if I were a hero—which I assure you I am not, I would agree with you, Miss Brandywine. Unfortunately, you seem to have charmed—or at the very least caught the fancy of—my godmother, so I imagine we shall rub together again in future. I shall, of course, do my best to ignore the fact that I find you to be the most charmingly exasperating female I have ever encountered in my life."

He lay the second shell before the first, a little closer to Miranda's cover. She caught her smile between her lips, forcing herself to frown. "Tell me, do you make it a practice to threaten to horsewhip and break to bridle all the females of your acquaintance, sir?"

"No, only you seem to evoke those passions in my breast, Miss Brandywine. Your unfortunate penchant for being precisely where you do not belong is most—unfeminine."

Miranda placed her shell opposite his, close to his cover. As she carefully slected another from the pile, her eyes narrowed.

"Mr. Hartley considers me to be very feminine. And Mr. Hartley's opinion is the only one that interests me," Miranda responded coolly. She propped her chin in her hands and watched Marle's selection of another shell.

"I cannot, of course, judge Mr. Hartley's tastes. He is a poet, and we lesser mortals must always bow to the artist's genius. Both you and Mr. Hartley have lived abroad for a good space, and perhaps that may account for our differences. In England, it is hardly the custom for young ladies to frequent smugglers' dens, or to be so—well, forceful in their attitudes as you appear to be, Miss Brandywine." He dropped his shell to one side of the arrangement, leaning back in his chair to contemplate the effect.

"Then things must be very dull for young ladies in England," Miranda replied thoughtfully. "Perhaps very dull for all concerned." She laid her shell on the opposite end of the arrangement and selected another. "It seems that one is always being hedged in by the demands of propriety and custom. The only career open for a young lady is marriage, and to that end, she must always be subjugating her own opinions, her own personality and even her own heart to the demands of others. First, her Mama, and then her husband. And the alternative to marriage—a life as a spinster sister without funds, property or even the education to embark upon an occupation that might support her independently—is too gruesome for contemplation."

"You sound like a bluestocking, Miss Brandywine."

Miranda shook her head. "No, like you, I am merely realistic—and perhaps cynical. I have never liked to see a female forced into a marriage solely for material concerns. And yet, it happens all the time."

"Consider then, that after a time, a man is placed in a situation where he must marry, he must provide an heir, he must have a wife who will be able to carry on the traditions into which he was born. He must look about him carefully, and with the uneasy feeling that the pair of them are no better than breeding stock. The female to whom he proposes must meet certain qualifications of breeding, of an awareness of her duties as hostess and chatelaine. She must be able to provide him with children, and if not precisely love him, at least adapt a compliance toward her position. It is not a simple matter, but one goes about it with the same sort of knowledge one chooses one's heifers."

Miranda's eyebrows went up sharply, but she was forced to see that he was sincere. "Then you dislike all females so much that you could choose a wife so coldly?" she asked curiously.

Marle shrugged his elegant shoulders. "On the contrary, Miss Brandywine, no one could admire the fair sex more than I. But I am a Runford, and there are certain traditions that must be maintained. It is necessary that I marry and—well, I hope Miss Rockhall will not regret becoming a countess in time. I can offer her a great deal, and I think that with training, she may be made into a credible Lady Runford. The advantage to choosing a schoolroom miss is that she has not yet had time to develop the simpering, calculating manners of most of the predatory females one encounters at Almack's. And once we are married I imagine that we shall both do as we please, discreetly, of course, but—" He broke off and smiled at Miss Brandywine. "But I do not mean to bore you. I must marry, and I believe that Miss Rockhall will not regret her decision. I can offer her a great deal, after all."

"Your godgift from Lady Denham must have been your arrogance," Miranda said acidly, dropping her shell into place.

Marle smiled sunnily. "We Marles are an arrogant lot. Almost as arrogant as the Brandywines, I imagine. But come, Miss Brandywine, I dislike arguing with females. The fair sex, you will admit, appears in a most unflattering light when engaged in debate. The female mind is not equipped for logic, but for emotion. Your insistence upon disputation ill becomes you." He selected a shell and placed it before the last one she had moved, his smile lazy and amused. "If you continue in your present attitudes, I very much fear that people will say Mr. Hartley lives under the cat's paw."

From beneath the rim of her bonnet, Miranda stole a sharp glance at Marle, unable to decide if he were in jest or not. The afternoon sun slanted across his face, throwing his rough features into soft chiaroscuro. The yellow light illuminated his reddish blond hair into a soft halo about his long face, and his eyes crinkled into what could have been a frown or a smile. Vincent, she thought, is a proper name for him.

"Indeed, sir! And doubtless they shall say that my poor cousin has been browbeaten into submission to your arrogant pride, also!" She retorted. "I may only hope that your arrogance precludes such indiscretions!"

"I am guilty of many crimes, Miss Brandywine, but gossip is not among them. That is best left to your own sex."

"From my own experience with the military, men have no hesitations in ripping the character of others into shreds with a vehemence that a female would never dream existed."

"Only, my dear Miss Brandywine, because women are so much more practiced and subtle at that vicious art than men," Marle responded, rising to his feet.

Without a nod, he leaned over Emily and whispered something in her ear that made her blush to the roots of her hair. Nodding to Lady Denham and the rest of the company, he leaned across the table and selected a large shell from the pile, smiling at Miranda.

"I shall hope that you dance as well as you debate, Miss Brandywine, for I shall expect you to place my name upon your card for the Wednesday Assembly— the second waltz." He bowed, placed his crown beaver upon his head and placed the large shell over the arrangement on the table as if making a checkmate.

CHAPTER SEVEN

It was one of those bright spring days that are particularly salubrious at the seaside. Up and down the white marble sweep of Marine Parade scullery maids were scrubbing down the steps, grooms were bringing around hacks for morning rides, coachmen drawing up their vehicles before doorways where ladies and gentlemen would soon emerge, after a hearty breakfast, for a pleasant drive through the landscape just beginning to blossom into the lush foliage of summer; butchers' boys and bakers' 'prentices were delivering their goods to housemaids belowstairs, perhaps stopping for a few minutes of mild flirtation, a pleasant truancy for the day's chores that Russet, normally a high stickler to rival Lady Denham, found to be a seasonal spectacle as reassuring as the swallows that sang in the trees along the walk. Only the postboy's horn provided a musical theme to this vernal symphony of sights and scenes.

Russet, having laid out the ladies' breakfasts and assured himself that the staff were all gainfully occupied upon their day's activities, had seized upon this brief moment to catch a breath of the air, while polishing the brass knocker upon his mistress's front door. Even the most well-regulated butler must be permitted his moments of reflection upon the microcosm of his ordered universe. And who could blame him, as he busily applied his soft flannel to the gleaming lion's head (a chore he would never entrust to a footman) for thinking briefly that if Parliament's houses were regulated with such attention to detail and order as Lady Rockhall's household, well, that England would be all the better for it?

From the inner pocket, he withdrew his watch (a gift from the late Lord Rockhall, to commemorate fifteen years of faithful service to the Family) and glanced at the time. Ten o'clock precisely. Lady Rockhall's abigail would be knocking upon her bedchamber door with her chocolate, and the young ladies would just be rising from the breakfast table and proceeding to the morning room, where a copy of the *Post* had been thoughtfully laid out upon the table. Mrs. Pymm would be sorting linens in the closet, and since it was Tuesday, George would be polishing the silver, while Alphonse, having labored over breakfast, would be preparing for luncheon. A well-regulated household, Russet thought with satisfaction, using his little finger to bring up the shine on each individual tooth of the grinning brass lion.

"Good morning, Mr. Russet, and a fine morning it is, I might make so bold as to add," the postboy said cheerily, touching a finger to the brim of his cockaded hat as he handed over the mail packet into the butler's care.

"Good day, Jerry, and indeed it is," Russet unbent

so far as to reply, thumbing expertly through the packet of fashion journals, sealed epistles, and elegantly scripted invitations. "There is nothing quite so beneficial to the general welfare as sea air, upon such a day," he added generously.

The postboy nodded respectfully, and continued on up the street, whistling to himself.

Tucking his dusting cloth over his arm, Russet glanced casually through the stack of invitations. Since the arrival of the young ladies, such missives had been on the increase, and it was a part of his unofficial duties to tactfully prod Lady Rockhall into responding to such invitations, remind her of the dates of her engagements and see that she arrived at her destination within a reasonable span of the appointed time. Thoughtfully, Russet narrowed his eyes, for it was coming near the time that Lady Rockhall must think of having her own entertainments, for the Season was fast coming upon Sanditon, and the town was thick of company. It would not do for Number Four to be behindhand in polite society. And, of course the young ladies must be formally presented. Anticipation of precisely the sort of occasions that Russet felt displayed his skills to the best advantage made the butler feel even more expansive toward the day.

From the morning room there lifted the vague, sweet strains of Miss Rockhall's nimble fingers upon the keys of the pianoforte, and Russet paused for yet a second longer to savor the joyful cleverness of a Bach sonata. Truly Miss Emily had a gift for music above the normal schoolgirl's piddles—her fingers seemed to coax magic from Lady Rockhall's ancient box. It was, Russet thought serenely, a perfect touch to a well-regulated morning. God was indeed in his heaven, and all was right with the world.

At that moment, Russet happened to spy a familiar

figure making its way up the pavement, and his pleasure turned to bile.

Mr. Hartley, oblivious to the admiring stare of a lady's maid walking a small dog, strolled along the paving stones, his blue eyes seeing only some interior vision, How else, Russet thought with resignation, to rationalize the way in which his raven locks curled about his brow in no known style of masculine hairdressing? What other possible explanation could there be for the disaster of a more-Byronic-than-Byron collar, shirtpoints sadly wilted, kerchief tied askew in such a way as to expose a great deal more of his neck (and chest!) than Russet felt entirely necessary, even for a poet? But what excuse could there be for such an unpressed coat of blue broadcloth, worn with a pair of fawn-colored breeches just scraping the tops of a pair of very scuffed shoes? Of Mr. Hartley's waistcoat, Russet refused any contemplation at all; it was enough to see the familiar and unwelcome figure heading in the direction of *his* household to set his teeth on edge. Mrs. Pymm and the kitchen maids might sigh belowstairs that Miss Brandywine's young man was the handsomest, most romantic gentleman ever seen in Sanditon, and Russet might feel outraged betrayal at finding his most trusted footman seeking to imitate Mr. Hartley's Byronic collars, but Russet was unmoved. Now, take a gentleman like Miss Emily's Lord Marle, he thought regretfully; nothing of the fop or the dandy about him, but his clothes were neat and his valet knew how to polish a pair of Hessians....

Mr. Hartley paused for a second on the street, lifting his face toward the sky. Across the street, a young lady and her maid paused in their tracks to observe him; their sighs were almost audible as they observed his classic profile caught in inspiration. From an interior pocket, the notebook and pencil emerged, and Mr. Hartey scribbled down some lines, his lips moving as he silently repeated them.

As swiftly as it had descended, the muse removed again. With a sigh, Mr. Hartley thrust his notebook back into his pocket and approached the steps of Number Four.

For several moments he paused, staring upwards through Russet, one foot upon the step, one hand upon the rail, until the butler felt constrained to say something.

"Good day, Mr. Hartley," he ventured coldly.

"Such heavenly music! She plays like an angel! I knew there was a reason I must come here today!"

Russet blinked, uncertain what to make of this pronouncement, as Mr. Hartley remained rooted to the spot, rapturous. As the piece finished with a coda, Charles' trance seemed to break. He blinked his long lashes and favored Russet with his smile. "Good day, Russet! I trust the ladies are at home?"

It was on the tip of Russet's tongue to reply that the scullery maids were giving music lessons to the boots, but his professional ethics were far too nice for such thoughts. "I believe the young ladies are in the morning room, sir, if you would care to follow me into the house—" he began in his most repressive accent, but at the moment, the door flew open and a vocal Maria, dressed in rigid black and issuing a stream of Portuguese orders to her mistress just behind her, emerged from the household. Miranda, in a walking dress of pale rose muslin trimmed at hem and neck with appliqué leaves of deeper tint and very dashingly caught at the mutton sleeves with drapes of the same shade, a white silk and straw bonnet tied over her dark curls displaying three roses of lavender to match her little leather slippers, and a mauve and lavender parasol lopped over one arm and her gloves in one hand, was remonstrating good-naturedly with her dresser in that same language

Apparently the bone of contention was a white and murex-purple silk shawl, which maid was trying, in the interests of the deadly English climate, to force upon her mistress's back, but the exact details of this interesting contretemps were never determined, as Miranda paused to deliver a peck upon her betrothed's cheek even as she was declining the contested square of silk to be placed upon her back. "Darling Charles, I didn't expect to *see* you," Miss Brandywine said briskly, drawing on her gloves and adjusting Mr. Hartley's tie without much success. "You really must not sleep in your clothes. They have people at hotels who will be more than happy to press them for you and shine your shoes, you know. When we are married, you must have a valet!" From her reticule, she removed a tortoise-shell comb and pulled it through his hair in a fashion resembling a nurse with a charge. "You've come at a very bad time, my love, you'll never imagine who arrived in Sanditon yesterday, but old Major Plum-Veasy and Mrs. Plumb-Veasy, they were stationed in Lisbon when we retreated from Coimbra—Lord, there was a time! But they've taken rooms at the Sussex Buildings on Olive Street, and I must needs see them! Should you wish to come? I know you will find it deadly dull, as the talk will all be of military things, and old times, and people you don't know, but I know they would like to meet my fiancé—at some other time."

Charles opened and closed his mouth. "But—I have finished my poem—epic verse upon the sea—dedicated to you—" he stammered. "I thought you might like to hear it, my dear—"

Miranda patted his cheek. "I'm so sorry, darling, but not right now. I know it's a very good poem, but I can't keep the Major and Mrs. Plum-Veasy waiting, you know! They are quite particular friends of Papa's and oh, I must hear all the news! Do you go on and read it to Emily! She adores your poetry, and she's quite hipped today—I'll be back soon!"

And with that, Miranda and maid swept down the stairs, still arguing in Portuguese, with the best humor possible to judge by the tones of their voices.

It was not at all what Russet was used to, young ladies kissing their gentlemen on the street, and maids who remonstrated with their mistresses and poets on the doorstep. Deeply offended, he reminded himself to speak to Lady Rockhall about such goings-on. Only the prospect of supervising an ongoing series of entertainments such as must outshine those of his arch rival Wescott of Denham Place restored his humor. But he did speak sharply to the underfootman he found lurking belowstairs when he should have been polishing the wineglasses.

Emily was rather moodily interpreting a particularly gruesome Scots ballad when Charles found her in the morning room. Her blond locks were wound about her face in simple bands, but a few errant curls framed her heart-shaped face, beautiful even in a pensive study. In contrast to Miranda's dashing style, she was plainly attired in a simple round dress of sprig muslin with only a bit of lace at the throat and two simple flounces at the hem to ornament her person. Her only jewelry was a plain gold locket on a long chain about her neck, and the green riband tied at the high waist of her dress had been turned. Caught up in her music, she did not hear his entrance, and Charles, struck by the softly lit study she made, hesitated to break the spell.

Her singing voice was not strong, but she had that purity of tone given to gentler voices, and an intuitive nuance that lent exactly the right shade of dramatization needed for ballad singing. At that moment, un-aware of any observer, and completely absorbed in her creation, she was able to be totally unself-conscious, completely at ease with herself and with the medium of her expression. Her long fingers moved skillfully over the keyboard, transmitting her energy in all the movements of her body, her head and shoulders bent forward, her spine curved into the instrument, moving with the expression of the music she conjured and coaxed from the ancient instrument. This was not the prim formal recital of a young lady forced to the key-board to display her accomplishments, but the fullest empathy of a young woman creating music from the heart and the soul of her being.

Charles, with that painfully sharp stab of empathy visited too infrequently upon those who follow the art-ist's craft, suddenly saw Emily Rockhall not as Mi-randa's shy, frightened cousin suffering from missish marital hysteria, but rather as a gently sensitive young woman of intelligence and grace whose confidence had somehow been distorted and suppressed beneath the tyranny of a family of forceful, domineering personal-ities. A naturally passive and reflective disposition had no defense against the bullying ways of the Rockhalls and the Brandywines. And the Runfords, he added, to himself.

Almost as if Emily had read his thoughts and felt encouraged to rebel, she stopped in the middle of the ballad and suddenly shifted into a demonic étude that he thought might have been Haydn, but played with such force and emotion that the master might never have recognized the piece for his own. Anger ripped out of the notes; the sounds she coaxed from the pianoforte were emotional expressions the composer had never intended for his mannered piece. Her face was trans-fixed, and she cast her entire body into the playing of the piece as if it were more an act of catharsis than the performance of music. Angrily, the bone-rattle of the melody made a *danse macabre* in the still air of the room. This was not the restrained tinkering of a schoolgirl's *accomplishment* but the full expression of an artist, Charles thought with vague, not unpleased revelation.

With that uneasy sixth sense that one is being observed unaware, Emily glanced up from the keyboard. Her eyes met Charles' for a single horrified second, and slowly her accustomed persona of reticence descended upon her again like a domino. Her features slackened, her cheeks filled with angry color and the long fingers suddenly lost their skill, descending upon the keys in one dissonant chord. She half rose from the chair, looking wildly about the room as if searching for an exit. "Oh—Mr. Hartley—I did not see—that is—you—quite by surprise—unaware—" she stammered, her hands concealing themselves in the folds of her dress as if to hide the evidence of some crime.

"No, please, Miss Rockhall—" Charles began, taking one hesitant step toward her, his hands held out, palms up, in a gesture of reassurance, "I—it is I who must beg your forgiveness! I did not mean to startle you—your playing, Miss Rockhall—I was quite captured—entranced—" Charles tugged at his careless collar, shaking his dark locks. "I am supposed to be a poet, and yet, when I must find the proper words, my tongue deserts me! Miss Rockhall, you play with the genius of an artist. Please believe me when I tell you that! I am enchanted! Oh, wretched words, to desert me now!"

Miranda, had she been present, would have briskly ordered her betrothed not to enact such a dreadful Covent Garden melodrama of a speech, but Miss Rockhall's retiring sensibilities were far more delicately sympathetic, and she halted in her retreating step, her ex-

113

pressive eyes widening in a most charming manner, the faintest ghost of a smile playing about her lips. "Mr. Hartley, I know you mean to be kind, but please do not feel that I must be flattered. I know that I am the merest dabbler—"

"No, no!" Mr. Hartley protested vehemently. "I swear to you that I would rather place a pistol to my head than cajole you with flattery! I should have announced my presence immediately, but I found myself entranced by your playing! Yours is a most rare gift, Miss Rockhall! A gift of the muse Calliope!" He added with poetic passion. "Pray continue—do not deprive me of such pleasure!"

Emily clasped her hands and shook her head. "Oh, no! I cannot. You see, if anyone is watching me, I—I fly quite into a panic, and my fingers twist and turn all over themselves—Mama becomes quite angry with me whenever I must play before company, and says that twenty guineas were wasted on my instruction, because I cannot perform in a sedate and ladylike manner, but must be all over the keyboard, and playing pieces that are far above people's heads. When I am alone, you see, it is very different, for there is no one to judge me, or tell me that if I only put half as much time into my dancing and deportment as I did into my music that I would not be so awkwardly shy and goosish in Society—"

"THAT for dancing and deportment!" Mr. Hartley said, snapping his fingers. "Any simpering miss with a fan can dance a few steps and make insipid conversation, but you, Miss Rockhall, have talent!"

"M. Framboise—my music master—said I had some ability," Emily admitted shyly. "He said that had I been born into different circumstances, and started my instructions at an earlier age, I might have been able to make my living in the concert halls. But even if that were so, I am far too terrified of audiences to make the attempt. It is something that I do for my pleasure only." A rather melancholy look passed over her face. "Lord Marle, my fiancé, does not care for music either. He says that having three sisters who pound upon the pianoforte and hammerfinger at the harp and squawk in the most bansheelike fashion has quite given him a distaste for musical females."

"Then he is a philistine and a fool!" Charles exclaimed heatedly. "That is—forgive me, Miss Rockhall, I did not mean to speak ill of your intended, for Marle is possessed of many admirable qualities. He is brave, and accomplished as a sportsman, and—well, I am sure that he has many virtues."

"Yes, of course," Emily replied without much enthusiasm. "I am certain that he does. But I—" She bit her lip and gave her head a tiny shake, as if to reprimand herself for speaking too forwardly. "Mama says that he has many admirable qualities."

"Lady Rockhall seems to be a most—practical woman," Charles murmured.

Emily sighed. "Yes, I take after my father," she added vaguely. "Have you come to see Miranda? I fear you have missed my cousin. Some friends of the Brandywine's Spanish days are in Sanditon, and she has gone to pay a call upon them."

"So she informed me as she brushed past me on the steps. My dear fiancée, when she sets out upon some errand, is always in a great hurry to get to the place where she must be."

There was a brief period of rather uncomfortable silence, neither party meeting the gaze of the other. Never had the furnishings of Lady Rockhall's morning room received such admiring attention.

"Perhaps you would like to sit down. My grandmother should be coming downstairs very shortly. Admiral Arkwright generally arrives around this time of the morning to accompany her upon her promenade," Emily suggested.

"Admiral Arkwright!" Charles said in uneasy tones, thrusting his hands in his pockets and casting his glance about as if expecting to view that disapproving gentleman seated in some murky corner of the room.

"Yes," Emily replied, shifting uneasily by the pianoforte. "I'm so sorry that Miranda could not be here, but you know how very dull she finds Sanditon! I imagine it will make her happy to have friends here from her campaigning days."

"I had meant to read her the finished version of my poem upon the sea and moonlight," Charles sighed. "I thought, rather, that she might enjoy it. Miranda used to enjoy my poetry when we were in Vienna."

"I should like to hear it," Emily said quietly. Both hands flew to her cheeks. "Forgive me—I did not mean to—that is, if it is a poem that you have composed for Miranda—"

"Not at all. Should you really care to hear it, Miss Rockhall? Your appreciation for the rhymed verse is always deeply appreciated. You are a critic of sensitivity and discernment, you know."

"Oh, really," Emily said, shaking her head.

"Oh, no—I am quite sincere, I assure you," Charles replied. "I only wish that Miranda shared your—but of course, she has not been raised up to have a taste for the finer arts."

The clock on the mantel chimed the half hour, and Emily glanced at its ivory face. "Admiral Arkwright will be arriving at any minute—"

"Miss Rockhall, have you plans for this morning?" Charles ventured impulsively.

"Why, no. I meant to read a bit—one of Scott's novels

from the library—Gran'mama says it is quite amusing, but—"

"Then fetch your shawl and bonnet and let us stroll upon the shore. This day is far too lovely to be wasted within doors. After all, we both seem to find ourselves at loose ends, and, well, what harm can there be in sharing the pleasures of sea and sky upon such a day?"

Emily cast him a glance. "Oh, do you think it would be all right? The Admiral rather frightens me, and grandmother is always saying that I shall throw myself into the mopes if I dwell too long in the house—"

"Come," Charles ordered with a rare degree of mystery, and Miss Rockhall meekly obeyed.

Rather like two schoolchildren playing truant from their governess, the pair slipped out of the house only minutes before the Admiral's ponderous figure appeared at the doorway. As he raised his fist to the lion's head, his eyes narrowed upon the couple strolling down the cobbled walkway toward the sea.

"Hmm!" he said aloud.

"Pardon me, sir?" Russet asked as he opened the portals for my lady's most constant suitor.

Admiral Arkwright, his gold braid and medals as resplendently shining as Mr. Russet's doorknocker, started a bit. "What? Oh, er, good day, Russet! Her ladyship ready?" he asked, casually making his entrance into the house.

At that precise moment, Sophia's dresser was propelling her mistress, quite stylish in a Bath promenade costume of pine green and a bronze silk toque, down the stairs, just in time to greet her prompt companion. "Ah, Henry! There you are!" Sophia said briskly, "You see, Partridge, I told you there was no hurry, you see the Admiral has just arrived this minute—Russet, where are the young ladies? I should inform them that I am leaving," she said as she held out one daintily

117

gloved hand to her portly admirer and sought direction from her indispensable majordomo at the same moment.

"Miss Brandywine and her woman have gone to Olive Street to pay a call upon Major and Mrs. Plumb-Veasy, and Miss Rockhall is in the morning room with Mr. Hartley," Russet replied, handing my lady her bronze silk parasol.

"No she ain't," the Admiral said, propelling Sophia out the doorway before she could make further inquiries about this statement. Admiral Arkwright did not believe in airing one's laundry before servants, even such a toplofty servitor as Russet.

"Whatever do you mean, Henry?" Sophia inquired a little breathlessly as they descended the stairs. "She said quite distinctly last night that she would be going to visit these Plumb-Veasys on Olive Street—quite respectable people, I believe, friends of her father's—"

"It ain't Miranda I'm talking about, Sophie!" The Admiral, firmly placing his companion's hand within the crook of his blue serge and gold-braided arm, said, "Saw Miss Emily strolling down the street toward the ocean with that poet fella Miss Miranda's supposed to have in tow—arm in arm and laughing, just as neat as you please!"

"Fancy that!" Sophia said complacently, opening her parasol with one practiced hand. "Henry, is this not the beautiful day? Sanditon is truly filling with some interesting company. There is Lady Foote and that friend of hers, Miss Courtney, and Mr. Trevor, and the Baldcocks, and poor Maria Standish and that pack of daughters of hers—"

"Damn, Sophia, don't you hear what I say. That Hartley fellow and your granddaughter just skipped off to the beach together for all the world to see!"

"So you told me, Henry," the Dowager replied, bow-

118

ing slightly to a vague acquaintance in a laudulet rolling past. The Admiral tipped his hat with a smile he was far from feeling.

"Well, people are bound to talk! Both of 'em engaged to other people! I knew when those two gels descended upon you that it would lead to trouble!"

"Oh, Henry, don't be such an old nudgeon! There are probably upwards of a hundred people upon the sands today, and I daresay a good two-thirds of them are not engaged to anyone. Mr. Hartley may be a bit vague at times, but I am certain that they shall not be waylaid by highwaymen or pirates in broad daylight."

"But, my dear Sophia! To be seen, unescorted, in the company of another's intended—it was simply not done in our day!"

Sophia smiled. "Modern manners are certainly not all that they should be, but I would rather have young Hartley and Emily in a healthful stroll upon the beach than Viscount Marle and Miranda Brandywine placed together in a room, alone!"

The Admiral cast a suspicious look at his adored. "Sophie, what have got up your sleeve?"

"Why, nothing, Henry. I only wish to see both of my girls happily bestowed."

"We haven't had a moment's peace since those two gels descended upon your household!" the Admiral grumbled.

"No, and I must admit that I am vastly diverted by the change," her ladyship responded complacently, squeezing her companion's stout elbow a little harder. "After one has passed through the follies of youth, one first tries to warn the younger generation of the pratfalls which lie before them. And then when that does not succeed, one worries. And then, when worry does no good whatsoever, one learns to relax and enjoy it, rather like a very good play. Both of my girls have good heads and hearts, each in her own way. But, like all *la jeunesse,* they are blinded by their own inexperienced experience! Besides, my dear old friend, nothing but nothing would please me more than to throw a spoke into That Woman's wheel! I do have a considerable fortune of my own to bestow, you know... well, speak of the devil...."

The Admiral followed her glance to see the approaching figure of Viscount Marle, elegant in his quiet biscuit-colored pantaloons and chocolate-colored morning coat, strolling down the Strand with the slight, rolling gait of a man who spends a great deal of his time upon the seas.

"There's a fellow more like!" the Admiral said approvingly. "None of those die-away poetical airs about him!"

"And none of the sensitivity or understanding, either," Sophia replied.

Before the Admiral could inquire as to precisely what she meant by *that* remark, Sophia was graciously allowing the viscount to doff his high-crowned beaver from his gold locks.

"Good day, ma'am! Servant, Admiral! I see I have chosen a bad time to come calling. But I was hoping that I might have an interview with Miss Rockhall when I espied Miss Brandywine turning into Olive Street."

The Admiral hemmed, but Sophia smiled sweetly, perfectly aware of the double message contained in this sentence. "I fear you shall be disappointed upon both counts, then! Miss Rockhall and Mr. Hartley are taking a promenade along the beach. I could not tell you in which direction they are moving."

A rather interesting expression crossed the viscount's features. Exactly what it might mean, Sophia could not determine, but she was put in mind of her grandnephews when disappointed of some activity regarded with mixed feelings. "Ha," Marle replied thoughtfully. "I am somewhat vexed. I have not been able to pay my proper duties to Miss Rockhall since I put into Sanditon. My yacht has needed certain repairs which have required my supervision—I'm certain Miss Rockhall understands! But while paying my duties to my godmother, Lady Denham, the other day, I happened to meet the ladies and Mr. Hartley quite by chance at the tea pavilion, and Lady D. quite raked me over the coals for not being a more attentive fiancé." He smiled ruefully.

"My granddaughter has been quite fagged to death by the rigors of her London Season," Sophia replied smoothly, "and not at all able to face up to the strain of too many visitors. That Wo—I mean Emily's Mama overestimates her energy, I fear."

Mark shifted his weight. "I was hoping that she would consent to tour my yacht when her health permitted. As the future Lady Marle, she must, of course, accommodate herself to the craft, and issue what orders for change she must like, staff, refurbishing, the sort of thing that females must have." His voice was impersonal.

"Perhaps some time in the near future," Sophia suggested.

"Perhaps. She's with Hartley, did you say?"

Sophia nodded. "Such little promenades are exactly what must suit her constitution best. I heartily doubt that she would be up to the strain of even so much as a day's sea cruise, you know."

Marle nodded. "I see," he said stiffly. "Well, perhaps you will be good enough to tell her that I had come to call, and I shall hope that her delicate health will enable her attending the Assembly this evening?"

"Only for a very short time, I am certain. But yes,

we shall be there, Lord Marle. Good day; it was quite pleasant to see you again."

And with those words, Sophia and the Admiral continued their stroll.

Out of the corner of her eye, Sophia watched Marle pause upon the sea walk and survey the landscape of the beach, evidently without success.

"Six of one and half dozen of the other," she murmured to herself.

"Eh? What did you say, Sophie?" Admiral Arkwright asked, quite properly at sea in waters he did not understand.

"Oh, nothing, Henry. Nothing at all. Come, let us stroll past the Pump Rooms and see what new company has descended upon us. I should love to encounter Elizabeth Denham."

CHAPTER EIGHT

Due to the bulk and volume of gossip, news and experience that had passed since last Miss Brandywine had encountered the Plumb-Veasys, and their mutual pleasure in carefully analyzing every scrap of the past and present doings of themselves and others, it was quite late in the afternoon when Miranda returned to Marine Parade.

There, she found that her cousin was laying down upon her bed with a cold cloth upon her forehead, ostensibly as a result of too much exposure to the rays of the sun, or so the footman informed her, and Miranda, having little patience with such mild indispositions, when she had been used to the sort of hospital duty incurred in battlefields, was content to accept that explanation without seeking interview with her cousin.

Instead, she found Sophia closeted with Russet, a morocco-bound list of names and residences, a cluster of menus, vintners' lists, caterers' cards and orchestra programs, planning what the Dowager mildly informed her niece would be A Little Entertainment. Since this proposed gathering seemed to consist of over a hundred people that Sophia found impossible to exclude from something as small as a musical evening with a little dancing, and since that list was rapidly expanding even as Miranda inquired of what assistance she could possibly be to her aunt and the invaluable factotum, she was able to put her experience to good use for the remainder of the day planning floral arrangements and menus for the very select supper of thirty couples to precede the evening, making the choices of a pink tent in the garden or a bower of seasonal flowers and seashells, the proper amount and vintage of champagne and wine to be provided, lobster patties or crab tortes, and a hundred and one other decisions that must be made, planned, set into action and rejected for yet something else.

Russet, who had hitherto felt Miss Brandywine to be a trifle too continental in her manners for an unmarried lady, developed a certain grudging respect for her experience in planning entertainments. And Lady Rockhall, who was at best, indecisive, was relieved to find that her niece was willing to shoulder the blame and the responsibility for certain of the more daring innovations her ladyship would have liked to make. The waltz would be danced; pink tents were quite dreary since the Duchess of Richmond's famous ball upon the eve of Waterloo; only Princess Bourghes would be so common as to feature champagne fountains; and no one wanted to do anything like Pauline Bonaparte, did one? So *common,* after all. The vacationing American Consul and his wife were certainly good enough to be extended an invitation—she was deliciously witty in Ghent, and a certain very dull Carleton House personage rusticating temporarily in

Sanditon would never do, as it was known that in his cups he pinched the housemaids and attempted to lead the orchestra. A rather dashing widow would add some spice and balance a ponderously charitable vicar exactly. White and red tea roses would make up into a lovely centerpiece, and Naldi's Orchestra was far more the go than the Scots Pipes. This and a hundred other things made up the desultory, pleasant planning of the afternoon, and by the time Russet gently reminded the ladies that it was time to dress for dinner, the structure of the planned evening was quite secure. Over a rack of veal and only one or two removes of Russian salad and raspberry kit, however, the discourse was still of the party, and if Emily only poked her food about her plate and took little part in the general conversation, Lady Rockhall and Miranda barely took notice.

It was only later, when Miranda had left the capable hands of Maria and come into her cousin's room to offer her services, that Emily spoke.

Miss Rockhall, still in her stays and petticoats, was seated at her dressing table, her curling iron growing cold in her hand, her gown still wrapped in tissue upon her bed, staring moodily into the mirror.

"What, slowpoke! Not dressed yet?" Miranda exclaimed cheerfully. "Do you not feel well, my love?"

Emily started from her reverie. "Oh, no—it is not that—I feel perfectly well—oh, look at the time, and my hair not even done!" Emily wailed, rising in a rustle of silk petticoats from her seat and attempting to do everything at once.

Issuing Maria swift instructions in Portuguese, Miranda helped her maid spread out Emily's delicate gossamer dancing dress, and sent the abigail to press it in her own room, while she set to do Emily's curls herself.

As Miranda worked expertly with the irons and a

125

mouthful of hairpins, she began a rather amusing story about how she had learned to do up her own hair at a moment's notice in field camps near Corunna, and suddenly perceiving that her cousin was in some agitation, she lay down the brushes and irons and placed her hands upon Emily's shoulders. "What's the matter, little love? It cannot be all that bad."

"I must confess, Miranda," Emily said in a low voice. "I am the greatest wretch alive!"

Miranda, who could not imagine how her cousin could possibly fit this appellation (she knew several better candidates) shook her head slightly. "Whatever makes you say such a silly thing? Come, tell, they say confession is good for the soul," she teased.

"This morning, I took a walk upon the beach with Charles—Mr. Hartley," Emily confessed, hanging her half-curled head. "He had come to call upon you, but you had gone on to your friends, and Admiral Arkwright was coming, so we—we took a walk along the beach, quite unescorted! We walked for quite two miles! Oh, Miranda, I am so sorry!"

Miranda shook her head and smiled. "Sorry for what? Nothing could make me happier than to see my fiancé and my cousin getting along so famously. Did you have to listen to his poem? Was it quite so dull as I imagine?"

"Mr. Hartley's poetry is very moving," Emily replied a little stiffly, raising her head. "He is quite perceptive."

"As you say," Miranda answered indifferently, glancing at the clock. "Oh, you silly goose! How could I be jealous of either you or Charles? I love you both very much, and I am very glad that you rub together so well. I know Charles far too well to believe that he would conduct himself in any way that was improper—"

Emily shook her head. "Oh, no. Nothing improper at all. It is just that people do talk and I did not think that our walking out together could possibly be construed as anything but two people enjoying a fine day, but Sanditon is full of—"

"Dreadful old cats!" Miranda finished. "Come now, don't be so silly, little love! The English still amaze me! In Europe, no one would think a thing of two friends on a walk in a public place."

Emily was silent, and Miranda swiftly arranged her flaxen tresses into a very becoming Psyche knot about her crown, with loose tendrils framing her piquant face. Cajoling her into smiles, Miranda screwed pearl droplets into her cousin's ears and lightly touched her cheeks with rouge, then darkened her lashes with soot.

Sophia had just been turned out by the stolid Partridge in mauve crepe banded with deeper bands of violet silk to set off her famous amethyst *tremblant* ensemble when the cousins emerged from their chambers.

As she allowed her abigail to drape an ivory cashmere shawl over her arms, the Dowager surveyed her two charges critically. No one could find fault with Miranda's pomander silk dancing dress, striped with contrasting bands of peach and bunched at hem and decolletage with twisted braid of gold lamé exposing delicate *partiers* of ivory Brussels lace. The Portuguese maid had brushed her méduse curls until they shone beneath the candlelight and threaded a golden net band through their raven luster. She had chosen the simplest of gold ornaments to fasten about her neck and wrist, and a pair of coral stars depended from her lobes. Over her arm she had slung a reticule of Moroccan leather, and carried a fan of enameled *japonais* openwork.

Emily, in a pale blue silk laid over with an openwork slip of gossamer lace worked into a design of butterflies

127

and forget-me-nots, delicate cap sleeves slashed with
sky blue ribands held back with tiny knots of white,
the hem of her skirt caught by a series of white appliqué
butterflies laid against a deeper blue bordering, thin
white and blue striped slippers upon her feet and a
spangled shawl caught in her arms, her only jewels the
delicate pearls Miranda had added to her toilette, was
in contrast to her more dashing cousin, almost as ethereal as a fairy princess. The pale colors of her costume
set off her pastel beauty to perfection, and as she turned
for her indulgent grandmother's admiration, her shy
pleasure in herself seemed to complete her grace in a
very different way from the frightened child who had
arrived in Sanditon just beneath a fortnight ago.

Miranda, perfectly aware that she was possessed of
excellent taste, but little classical beauty, joined in her
aunt's praise for Emily with a heartfelt and somewhat
self-satisfied sincerity. But of course, it took very little
to show Emily off to advantage, she thought shrewdly,
tucking her cousin's white embroidered reticule on her
arm and handing her a pair of kid gloves. Perfect
beauty should only be displayed in the simplest of set-
tings; anything too elaborate detracts from the jewel
itself, she recalled, giving one last turn of her finger
to an errant blond curl before pronouncing her cousin
complete to a shade.

But, being Miranda, she did pause before the mirror
in the hallway to reassure herself that she was in perfect order before following her aunt and cousin out the
doorway into the warm evening.

The Assembly Rooms were as full as they could hold
when the ladies made their entrance to the strains of
a lively country dance already in progress, but as she
greeted the august Mr. Theobald and graciously accepted his compliments upon herself and her charges,
Sophia was aware of a sense of satisfaction. Though

there might have been many fair and interesting young maidens present, there was none quite so lovely or graceful as Miranda and Emily. Of course she was the smallest bit prejudiced, she reminded herself, but it did give her a definite sense of satisfaction to see that her charges' dance cards were rapidly filling up, even though there was no sign of either young lady's fiancé among the gentlemen present.

A gentleman of rather newly acquired town bronze immediately recalled himself to Miss Rockhall's notice as one of her rejected Almack beaux, while a fiercely mustached gentleman in an empty-armed hussar uniform attached himself to Miss Brandywine with the information that she owed him the dance he had lost at that famous interrupted ball of the Duchess of Richmond's.

"Well, Randa, Mrs. Plumb-Veasy says you're going to buckle that poet," the major said bluntly as he and Miranda bowed and turned through the steps of the dance.

Miranda laid her hand on top of her old friend's and glided through the block. "That's right, Tom. Do you wish me well, or are you like all the rest of the old regiment and think I've flung my gun after my cannon?"

The major's mustache moved thoughtfully. "Known you since you was in short skirts, Randa, and I was green-commissioned. Never thought that you'd buckle yourself to a civilian sort."

"Have you heard that Sir Francis is properly put out?"

"Ha! So that's why you're here! In exile, in exile, is it?"

"No, a hasty retreat. The general, finding his chief aide-de-camp on leave, may also find that he doesn't know how to pack his own supply trains."

"You and Sir Francis are much of a stubborn match,

Randa my girl, and I'd rather lose my other arm to Boney's cannon than place a wager upon the outcome of that one. What makes you so certain the general will cry craven?"

Miranda was about to smile and make some smug reply when the dance required her to turn again, and she suddenly caught the sight of two men in the doorway. Taken unawares, for a second Miranda studied Lord Marle and Mr. Hartley as if they were strangers, and was somewhat startled by her own reactions. Marle's rough features made an incongruous contrast with his elegantly cut black evening dress, and the way in which he obliviously received Mr. Theobald's attentions as his due, surveying the room with his bored, rather arrogant stare seemed to sum together his views of this provincial assembly. Mr. Hartley's features, as even and handsome as the head of a newly minted Greek coin, almost excused, and perhaps enhanced the artistic negligence of his dress. He was neither bored nor oblivious, but rather seemed to be absorbing the scene before him as a part of some drama enacted for the benefit of his muse. And, if every other female in the room might sigh for the fact that Miranda's breathtakingly handsome fiancé preferred diminutive dark females to tall auburnettes or voluptuous blondes, Miranda herself was startled to experience no such elation herself.

The feeling passed before she could give it analysis, and Miranda shook her curls lightly. "Oh, he will, I think, when he sees that I am determined," she said rather lamely, and forced herself to concentrate upon the difficult passages of the dance in progress.

Passing Emily, she managed to poke her cousin's arm with the point of her fan and signal with her eyes toward the doorway.

Emily completed the rondelet and returned to catch

Miranda's eye with an expressive glance. Miranda shrugged, as much at sea as her cousin as they parted again into the forms of the set.

Since they were both engaged to form the next set for the boulanger, the cousins had to sacrifice curiosity to propriety as they devoted their attentions to their partners and their steps. But Miranda watched with a certain vengeful glee as Mr. Theobald presented a very flirtatious schoolroom miss to Lord Marle, leaving the viscount no choice but to endure a full dance of her very forward and simpering mannerisms. She was, however, less pleased when the master of ceremonies presented Mr. Hartley to a particularly tall and stunning auburn-headed female known to be a recent and very well-off merchant's widow.

In fact, Mr. Hartley seemed to be enjoying this female's company entirely too much, Miranda decided as the dance ended, and with only the most perfunctory of applause, rather forgot all her well-laid intentions to protect Emily from Lord Marle as she lead her major away to reacquaint him with her fiancé and Mrs. Forbush. Fortunately, the young widow was more taken with a war hero in a dashing uniform than a poet in rather negligent evening dress, and Miranda was able to leave them together firmly in possession of her fiancé's hand for the first waltz.

"I was saving this dance for you, Charles," she said as the strains of the music began to float lightly across the floor. "The first waltz was always our dance."

Mr. Hartley smiled fondly down upon his diminutive sweetheart. "Were you indeed? It is much like Vienna, is it not? In fact, Miranda, you are trying to lead again."

Miranda gave a little sigh and relinquished control to Charles, who spun her gracefully across the floor. "My dear, that cravat is postively monstrous! When we are married, I shall have to engage a valet for you," she remarked, a little put out about his gentle criticism that she, Miranda Brandywine, was trying to lead. "How came you to fall in with Lord Marle?"

"Fall in with Marle? Ah, capital fellow, Marle. Interested in all the most progressive ideas. Uses gaslighting on his estate. Most progressive fellow I've ever known! Why, I was explaining certain theories of mine concerning the navigational use of the—"

"Oh, never mind," Miranda sighed. She was silent for a while, then threw back her head to look up at Charles' handsome chin. "Charles, did it ever occur to you how very *very* wrong he and Emily are for each other?"

"Miss Rockhall is a most estimable female, Miranda. Her sensibilities are finely tuned, and her appreciation of the arts is most nice. Took a walk with her today—she must have told you so—excellent creature, Miss Rockhall—"

"Yes, she is rather dear. But you know, I really don't think that she and Marle suit at all. He bullies her, you know! They are quite opposite in character!"

"People might say the same of us, my dear," Charles said. There was a distant, uneasy look in his blue eyes that Miranda did not catch, so intent was she upon her own train of thought.

"But we're different, Charles," she replied impatiently.

"Yes, I suppose we are," Mr. Hartley said after the most infinitesimal of pauses.

"When we are married—" Miranda begun, suddenly.

"I have finished a poem of which I am particularly happy—" Charles started to say.

This is nothing like it was in Vienna, they both thought silently.

* * *

"I hope you have saved the first waltz for your fiancé?" Marle asked Emily drily as he bent over her hand, shooting a meaningful glance at the young man who had just escorted her back to her place beside Sophia.

"I—that is—" Emily began, thrown into confusion as she turned from her partner to her fiancé.

But Marle was firmly leading her out upon the floor; his hand was upon her waist and he was looking at her in that way from beneath his heavy eyebrows. Inexorably, he was guiding her across the boards, with that faint, polite air of a man doing his duty.

"You are in fine looks tonight, Miss Rockhall," he ventured.

Emily nodded, miserably tongue-tied, as she always felt in his presence. "Thank you," she said in a small voice.

"You are very welcome," the viscount replied. "I trust you are recovering from the exhaustion of your London Season comfortably?"

"M-my grandmother takes very good care of me. And so does—my Mir—my cousin," Emily stammered. "I do-do not have to go out a great deal here."

"No. It is rather dull, I think."

"Oh, no! I do not think Sanditon is at all dull! It is very peaceful here with Gran'mama," Emily replied slowly. "It is what I am used to."

"So your grandmother gives me to understand," Marle replied, the faintest hint of amusement in his voice.

Emily lowered her eyes and did not respond. She bit her lower lip, with all the air of one who has received a sharp setdown.

When at last Marle ventured to speak again, it was with a more serious tone. "You and I have never spent any time alone, Miss Rockhall, not even since we have become engaged," he remarked.

"No, we have not," Emily agreed with some dread in her voice.

"Mr. Hartley and I were discussing the possibility of an outing on my ketch earlier in the evening. We agreed that a short afternoon's journey might prove amusing for you and Miss Brandywine. Would that meet with your approval? I promise I shall choose a day that is perfectly calm, and that if you show the faintest signs of *mal de mer*, we shall immediately return."

"Oh—I—that is, if Miran—Miss Brandywine agrees, I suppose I shall say yes also," Emily responded somewhat reluctantly.

"I would promise nothing too strenuous, in regard for your health, Miss Rockhall. Emily, if there is something on your mind, some thought you wish to place before me, I would be glad to listen. I am not an unfeeling ogre, you know," Marle said gently.

"Oh—I—" Emily began, suddenly heartened, but at that moment, the dance ended, and the couples upon the dance floor began to applaud the orchestra. Whatever Emily's response to this opening would have been was lost. With a small, ironic bow, Marle surrendered her to her next partner and retired toward the card room.

Emily sighed, vexed with herself, her eyes following him across the floor. If only she had a little courage, she thought bitterly, the whole thing might have been over and done with there!

Knowing that both her grandmother and Miranda would roundly castigate her for a want of courage, Emily did not confide this lost opportunity to either of her female relations. But Mr. Hartley, claiming his dance, was swift to note that his partner was valiantly concealing her distress.

"What is it, Miss Rockhall? Do you not feel well? It is far too hot in this room, I know," he said solicitously, his blue eyes peering into her own with tender concern, oblivious to the couples moving awkwardly around them.

Emily sighed. "Yes it is dreadfully heated in here—so many people—"

"Say no more! Let me take you out upon the balcony and procure you a glass of lemonade at once! Should you wish me to inform Lady Rockhall that you wish to leave?"

"Oh, no!" For then she and Miranda would be even more vexed with her—Gran'mama hated to give up her cards, and Miranda was having such a wonderful time. Emily managed a weak smile. "I shall be right as a trivet if only I may have some fresh air, I promise, Mr. Hartley."

It was the object of but a moment to see that Miss Rockhall was placed upon a chair on one of the balconies overlooking the Strand and the sea, a shawl draped about her shoulders against the warm night air and a glass of tepid lemonade brought to her hand.

After reassuring himself that she was not faint, nor cold, nor overheated, nor overexcited, but was indeed comfortably situated, Mr. Hartley placed himself opposite her upon the balustrade and regarded Emily with concern as she sipped at her potion.

"Forgive me for intruding, Miss Rockhall, but I see that you are in a considerable state of agitation. Indeed, I have noted that you have been laboring beneath some burden since first I met you. Can you trust the ear of one who hopes to call himself your friend?"

These words made Emily sigh, and one large tear glittered on her smooth, pale cheek. "Oh, Mr. Hartley, I am the most wretched creature alive!"

"Whatever would make you say that, Miss Rockhall?

You are certainly no wretch in my eyes. Indeed, i
would seem to me that you are blessed with every
grace—Lord Marle must consider himself a fortunate
man indeed to have won such a divine being for his
wife!" Charles declared passionately.

This caused a small torrent of tears from Miss Rock
hall. Mr. Hartley, the most chivalrous of gentlemen
was swift to offer both a well-made shoulder and a
slightly crumpled handkerchief, since the bit of lace
Miss Rockhall carried for this purpose was ineffectual
Without thinking, she leaned her head against Charles
chest and gave vent to her tangled emotions while
Charles, bemused, patted her shoulder and sought to
reassure her that whatever the problem, he would be
willing to move heaven and earth to find a solution.

The vision of Mr. Hartley, shoulder to the skies, laboring like a drayhorse to adjust the universe upon her
behalf made Emily giggle a little, and Mr. Hartley was
encouraged to detect a faint smile from beneath the
shower of tears.

Very gently, he took her hand into his own, and to
forestall any further torrents, spoke to Emily very quietly. "You must regard me as you would your own
brother, and consider me at your disposal, Miss Rockhall. Whatever is in my power to do, I shall endeavor
to perform for you."

"I ought to consider myself the luckiest female alive,
and yet I am so wretched," Emily sniffled. "And tonight,
he all but asked me if I wished to cry off, and—and I
lacked the courage to tell him that we should not suit!"

Vague enlightenment was beginning to dawn upon
Charles' consciousness, and he squeezed Emily's hand
within his own. "You do not wish to marry Lord Marle?"

Emily shook her head violently. With very little encouragement, he was able to procure the whole story

from her, and his poetic heart was outraged by the bitter injustice of it all.

"It is not that he is precisely the monster I thought him to be—I see that now, but he *still* frightens me so—and I don't wish to be a viscountess and have to preside over that enormous house and all those servants, and have to ride to hounds and sail on that yacht—and have to try to make conversations with his friends and his family—they are all so *tonnish*, and I am not at all—and, oh, I could not even muster the courage to tell him that I had made a mistake and we would not suit when he did everything but ask me if I had second thoughts tonight! I am a wretched coward, but when I think about Mama and how unpleasant she will be if I cry off, and then I think about how impatient Miranda and Gran'mama will be if they find that I had an opportunity and did not, and oh, I wish I were not such a wretched coward, but I do so much dislike people being cross and quarreling with me—I get quite nervous, and, and—" Miss Rockhall broke off and blew her nose. "I know Miranda would never get herself into such a situation. *She* would come cross as crabs right back at Mama and go on about her way!"

"Miranda and Sir Francis do quarrel in the most discomfiting manner, it can put one right out," Mr. Hartley admitted. "And yet, I believe that they both enjoy it!"

"There! You see? I know I am spineless, and entirely too passive, but when people press me so, I wilt! I cannot argue with them—I can only cover my head and tremble!" Emily said woefully. "Yet, what can I do, Mr. Hartley? I am quite miserable."

"For my opinion, I find Lord Marle in general to be an admirable man in his own fashion, but entirely too set upon his own consequence—yes! However, his entire family is like that, and I daresay he doesn't mean

137

to frighten you! He must have a sincere regard for you if he offered marriage."

Emily shook her head. "He only wants a wife. He must marry and have an heir, and he tells me that ours will be a union of convenience only!"

"Well, I imagine he meant it in the kindest way, but Marle doesn't seem to reckon with your sensibilities, Miss Rockhall."

"What am I to do? Mama says if I do not marry him that she shall have wasted all the money it cost to bring me out, and there are still my sisters to be provided for, and my brothers and—"

"And what of you, Emily? What do you want?" Charles asked her gently.

Emily looked away out across the water. "Once, you know," she said quietly, "I believed that some day, I should meet a gentleman who was very kind, and very understanding, who felt about things—music and books and quietude—in the same way that I do. But you see, since I have been quite fifteen or so, Mama has instructed me to put such silly thoughts out of my head and think only of my duty toward her and the family. Romance, she says, is not for people like us."

"Your mother is perhaps a great deal too practical. She cannot ask you to marry where every feeling is repulsed. It is clear that you and Marle would not rub together at all. I wish that there were something I could say to him—some word I could put into his ear that would convince him that you do not wish to enter into an engagement that—"

Slowly, Emily turned her head toward Charles, until their faces were but a few inches apart. Mr. Hartley's words trailed away. He was only conscious of the scent of Miss Rockhall's light perfume and the touch of her hand in his own. Emily raised her face toward his and closed her eyes with a little sigh.

"Sweet Emily, when beheld by moonlight," Mr. Hartley, or rather his muse, whispered, but he was reluctant to let go of her hand and search for his notebook.

Emily's long lashes fluttered open and she stared at Charles for a long time, her green eyes infinitely sad. "Charles," she breathed.

"Emily," he responded, intoxicated.

"Dear Charles..." Emily murmured gently. "Miranda..."

With a long sigh, Mr. Hartley disengaged his hand from Miss Rockhall's. "Yes, Miranda. Quite so," he said, as if from a long distance away. "I am certain that she will contrive to straighten things out for you, with Lord Marle. Miranda is very good at managing things..."

"Yes. She is very dear to me. I would not hurt her for the world," Emily said, straightening out the fringes of her shawl.

"Indeed, Miranda is a paragon of virtues. And you must think of Lord Marle, Miss Rockhall. The advantages he can offer you should certainly not be cast aside lightly—title, position, family—All I possess is a small estate, my expectations are not large, you know. Upon the death of an aunt, I shall inherit a small house and a bit of land, but is as nothing compared to the glories of Runford Place. At least Miranda thinks it is not very much."

"Of course, the Brandywines have a very pleasant house in Devon.... Miranda is Sir Francis's only child...."

"Yes. Miss Rockhall, you shall always have my deepest esteem and my friendship, you know..."

Emily touched his hand lightly, sadly. "And you shall always have mine, Mr. Hartley," she replied gravely.

"Shall I see you to your grandmother?"

"If you would be so kind, Mr. Hartley—" Emily managed a weak smile. "You are—very kind!"

139

"And you are the most wonderful of females, Miss Rockhall."

Still, they lingered on the balcony, unable to face one another, and yet still unable to part, staring across the infinite waves of the rolling ocean.

Breathless and laughing, Miranda had just completed a lively dance with a young naval officer when she felt a touch upon her shoulder.

Lord Marle made his slight, ironic bow. "This is my dance, I believe, Miss Brandywine?" he asked.

The laughter half faded from Miranda's face. "Oh," she said, glancing at the card attached to her wrist, her brows drawing together slightly. "So it is. I forgot that I had promised you—or rather, that you had commandeered the second waltz from me. You will forgive me, Lieutenant FitzClarence?" she asked with a breathy smile for her erstwhile partner. The young man bowed reluctantly, and Marle firmly marched his prize away.

"High-handed!" Miranda teased him quizzically. "I must thank you for putting down your cards and coming to honor your promise! That particular member of *les Bâtardesses* is as clumsy as his father! I wonder where Mrs. Jordan's graces went with him?"

"Vixen!" Marle said without rancor, spinning her about the floor. He danced, Miranda thought, with proficiency, but without the grace of Mr. Hartley. Still, he did not tread on her toes, and it was quite nice to be held in so strong an arm and propelled just so.

"I imagine you had quite another species of female animal in mind, Lord Marle," she replied.

"On the contrary, Miss Brandywine, I am quite fond of animals." Marle's grin flashed wickedly. "It is *people* who arouse my ill-natured sensibilities!"

Miranda made a *tsk*-ing noise, shaking her head.

"You must have been losing at the pasteboards, milord. Dipped upon chicken-stakes?"

"Would that it were so! Your aunt has roundly taken me upon guinea points. Even now I imagine she is counting up her wins and planning how best to spend her newfound fortune! Will it be an ermine cloak or an emerald tiara?"

"She has an emerald tiara, and a perfectly dreadful thing it is, I might add. So, you've contrived to put ermine upon her back, and I wish her well for so roundly touting you, if you have been so foolish as to play for guineas with Aunt Sophia. With your amazing powers of insight, I was certain you would recognize the hardened faro's daughter lying beneath that deceptively fragile nature. Aunt *always* wins!"

"I left my godmother in my seat, determined to recoup the family honor," Marle laughed. "Lady Denham is a cutthroat player, you know. Besides, what I have lost in chachwheels, I am certain to gain in Lady Rockhall's good graces."

Miranda shook her head. "You are totally without conscience or manners! No, don't remind me—you have told me so time out of hand of that fact."

Marle looked down at Miranda, shaking his head. "Exasperating! But her ladyship's good graces are important to me, you know."

"But not, it seems, her granddaughter's," Miranda replied thoughtfully, inclining her head with a slight smile for a passing acquaintance.

Marle's heavy brows lifted slightly. "Why do you say that? I presume you mean Miss Rockhall?"

"I notice that you have only stood up with Emily once this evening."

"Hm! I suppose you're correct. Not a dancin' man, really. Though of what interest it could possibly be to you, Miss Brandywine, I cannot fathom."

141

"You cannot put my nose out of joint, Lord Marle, by giving me a setdown upon the Paul Pry! There are many voices to tell my cousin what she must do and how she must do it, but it seems to me that there are very few ears listening to what she wants to do!"

Marle looked thoughtful. "Why do you feel Miss Rockhall needs a champion, Miss Brandywine? And why have you placed yourself in that role? It is hardly the sort of part I would cast you in, the protector of your shy cousin."

"Perhaps I am not as selfish as you seem to believe I should be, Lord Marle. Is that another characteristic of the homegrown English female? I shall have to remember it, I see. It certainly answers the question of why no one else will speak for Emily."

"And what does Emily have to say that she cannot voice for herself?"

Miranda suddenly realized that she had allowed her tongue to run her into a trap where she was surrounded on three sides. "Why don't you ask her?" she finally replied innocently with a smile she was far from feeling. Truly, rescuing Emily was getting deeper and deeper into the war, when all she had intended were one or two swift guerrilla thrusts to demoralize the enemy.

"Do you know," Lord Marle was saying pleasantly, "I find Mr. Hartley to be a most amiable fellow, when he is not under your influence. It is indeed fortunate that his mind is of an elevated nature, else I dread to think what your meddlesome manners and your intriguing wiles might wreck upon his unsuspecting person, Miss Brandywine."

"Checkmate, Lord Marle—for now," Miranda said with a great deal more treacle than honey in her voice.

"For now, Miss Brandywine. Are we once again agreed that we disagree about everything?"

Miranda sighed. "I wish it were not so, Lord Marle," she said frankly.

"Do you know, Miss Brandywine, that is one thing that we may agree on?"

Two pairs of eyes met. With rather more force than he might have intended, Marle turned his diminutive partner about on the floor in such a way that her body drew a little closer to his own. Almost reluctantly, she relaxed and allowed herself to follow his lead. From beneath half-closed eyes, Miranda permitted herself a little smile, and was rewarded with a grin from Lord Marle that was, for once, completely without irony or malice. And perhaps not even a trace of that infamous arrogance.

"What are you thinking about?" Marle asked Miranda, after a time.

Miranda opened her eyes. "Do you know, no one ever asked me that before?" she said slowly.

"I admit it is an unusual question."

"I wondered what *you* were thinking about," Miranda countered.

"Ah," Marle said. "My thoughts, Miss Brandywine, would never bear your clever scrutiny." He hummed a snatch of the gay waltz music. "I hope that you sail as well as you dance, Miss Brandywine," he said cryptically.

CHAPTER NINE

Miranda was no great admirer of music. A succession of governesses had tried and failed to coax recognizable tunes from her sullen fingers on the harp or the pianoforte; even her dearest friends admitted that her voice could not carry a song in a knapsack, and Mr. Hartley was always vaguely scandalized at the number of very improper soldiers' ballads that comprised her repertoire. The stirring martial strains of a military band at parade review, a danceable waltz or boulanger and certain very light music hall ballads were all that really had the faintest appeal to her; and these must needs serve only as the background to some occupation far more active than listening for her not to squirm with impatience.

But discreetly squirming she had been all that morning in one of Sophia's nile-green morning-room chairs while Emily at the pianoforte and Charles with his guitar amused themselves with a series of popular ballads of such a dreadfully Gothic nature as to make Miranda feel quite *hipped.* In her lap lay a portfolio of Mr. Hartley's poetry which she was ostensibly reading. Concealed behind the tall bound covers, however, she had managed to secret the latest copy of *La Belle Assemblée,* but even the prospect of fuller sleeves and deeper hems for the coming season could not keep her eye from wandering from time to time toward the open window, where a warm summer day seemed to be gloriously forming itself from an indifferent morning.

Sophia, perhaps wisely, had not yet issued from her chambers, and the presence of M. Alphonse, her very temperamental hairdresser, promised that her absence from the scene would last until either luncheon was announced or the current store of gossip completely aired and dissected.

Miranda propped her chin in her hand and watched without rancor as Emily and Charles good-naturedly argued the proper key in which both could sing a particularly (to Miranda) loathsome ballad concerning the drowning of some nameless maiden by her faithless lover. Miranda thought the wretch deserved it for being so silly as to get herself into such a condition in the first place, but both Miss Rockhall and Mr. Hartley seemed to regard the sad ballad as particularly emotionally rending, to judge from the rather melodramatic way in which they were regarding one another as they played and sang.

As Mr. Hartley leaned over to turn the page of the sheet for Emily, some vaguely uneasy thought crossed through the bored recesses of Miranda's mind, but before she could dredge this image up into the light for a closer mental inspection, Russet announced the presence of Lord Marle.

The viscount's entry, had Miranda not been too relieved to escape from her ennui to notice, cast an unsubtle change over the musicians. Emily's fingers froze upon the keyboard, and a crimson flush rose up from the neckline of her sprig muslin morning dress as she rose to greet her fiancé. Mr. Hartley tugged uneasily at his Byronic collar and separated his distance from Miss Rockhall by a good extra yard. Neither looked at the other, and Emily managed a tolerable composure at facing her nemesis, while Charles thrust his hands into his pockets and nodded affably.

Marle, as usual, looked a trifle incongruous in his impeccable attire. This morning, he wore a champagne hacking jacket and lustrous top boots, a blue kerchief knotted over his shirtpoints.

"Marle," Miranda said with a great deal more enthusiasm than she meant to convey.

Reluctantly, Emily, risen from the pianoforte, bowed toward her fiancé, murmuring about pleasant surprises.

With his accustomed formality toward his intended, Marle bent over her hand, complimenting her upon her color, which had the effect of deepening her blush by several tones. He nodded in Miranda's direction with a slight, ironic smile, and affably hailed Mr. Hartley. "I see I have interrupted your music-making. Pray do not allow me to hinder you—continue on, if you please."

Emily clasped her hands together. "Oh, no, we were finishing just as you came in, were we not, Mr. Hartley?" she asked in a small voice, looking toward Charles for reassurance.

Unconsciously, Mr. Hartley drew a little closer to her, his clear blue eyes almost challenging as he looked down upon Marle. "As Miss Rockhall says, we were almost finished, Marle."

The viscount nodded. "What a happy group you make, Miss Rockhall and Hartley making their music and Miss Brandywine reading?—"

146

Miranda closed the book swiftly. "Just some poetry of Charles'," she said, certain that he had seen the concealed periodical in the pages of the portfolio.

"Thinkin' of publishin', Hartley?" Marle asked, retrieving the folio from Miranda's lifeless fingers and paging through the leaves. Miranda held her breath, rather glaring at Marle, certain that he would pull the journal from its hiding place, but he closed the covers and laid it upon the table. "No end to your talent is there, old man?" the viscount asked Charles with a smile. "Ain't a reading man myself, but I like to think that I recognize what's good. Speakin' of which, have you made any progress with the nautical compass?"

Charles, unused to praise, pushed his hands into his pockets and took a deep breath. "I am working with the gauges—to create some sort of easily read indicator is—"

Miranda, recalling the infamous and unfortunate demonstration of Charles' gas lanterns in Vienna, wisely, she decided, intervened. "Charles, I am certain that Lord Marle does not care to hear the details of your experiments. All this scientific progress is, I believe, flying in the face of safety and well-being! Do you know that they say these new steam engines will pull a carriage at twenty miles an hour? Why people shall be crushed by such speeds!"

Charles looked slightly downcast, but Marle smiled again. "No sense in borin' the ladies, Hartley! Female minds ain't suited to mechanical principles after all. We'll discuss it later."

Miranda, aware that she had been subtly put in her place, frowned and crossed her arms across her bodice, but said nothing.

Forestalling the uncomfortable silence that was bound to ensue, Marle turned toward Emily. "Miss Rockhall, it is you that I have come to call upon today!

147

My boat's still in the hands of the chandlers, Lady Denham's entertaining the missionary society and I've been reduced to hiring the best hacks I could find in Sanditon. I should have had my own cattle brought down, had I known that I would be staying this long in town, but I hope you will allow me to make do with what I could find and do me the honor of riding out to Brinshore with me today."

Emily looked stricken. "You know—not a good horsewoman," she said in a very small voice, casting an imploring look at Miranda.

Miss Brandywine was equal to the breach. "What a capital idea, Marle!" she said briskly. "Charles and I were thinking of making that same trip! We may make a party of it!"

Charles felt an uncomfortable little fist digging into the small of his back. "What? Oh—of course," he said uncertainly. "Brinshore. Interesting place. Quite historical. Old cathedral there worth seein'."

Since none of the party had the faintest idea of what was to be offered by the neighboring hamlet of Brinshore, this remark was allowed to pass unremarked upon.

"And," Miranda continued quickly, "since Emily is somewhat afraid of horseback riding, I am sure that it would be a simple matter to rent a gig from the livery stable—Charles is an excellent whipster!"

Since Mr. Hartley was only the mildest sort of driver, he cast an astonished look at Miranda, but she rushed onward rather breathlessly.

"I am dying to ride! Aunt keeps no horses, you know, so I have been bound to only get my exercise by walking or sea bathing—shall we all take our bathing costumes, do you think? What a capital idea, Marle."

Miranda missed the frosty smile the viscount bestowed upon her when she glanced toward Charles with an imploring expression. "Quite so," he murmured. "But perhaps we may simply content ourselves with a picnic lunch. I hope there are high, rocky bluffs in Brinshore with steep, sharp drops into the sea."

"Oh, so do I!" Miranda continued blithely, not quite liking herself for this necessary degree of *coming,* but feeling obliged to defend her own motives. "I do so like a scenic view."

Marle made a sound that might have been a snort, and Miranda had the grace to blush.

"It—it sounds very nice to me," Emily suggested timidly, casting a despairing look at Charles, who was looking from Emily to Miranda with some understandable feeling of confusion.

Marle sighed. "It is decided then. Hartley, shall you contrive to rent a gig?"

"That shall be wonderful," Miranda said. "It will only take a second for Emily and me to change, and we may procure a luncheon from Alphonse, I think."

Marle gave Miranda one of his short, ironic bows. "Exasperating," he murmured under his breath.

"Just so," Miranda said sweetly. "Shall we all meet here in an hour?"

This being agreed upon, the company parted, but not before Miranda was able to draw Charles a little aside and press her message home.

"Dearest, I know how very difficult all of this must look to you, but please bear a little understanding—this is merely a tangle that I must try to unknot for Emily—but it is imperative that she is not left alone in Marle's company."

Charles looked a little astounded, but since he was perfectly used to Miranda's managing ways, and knew very well Emily's reasons for not wanting to be alone with Marle, made no demur, merely assured his beloved that whatever arrangements she wished to make were perfectly fine with him, and wandered off with Marle with some vague idea that he was to engage a gig from the livery stable at the Sanditon Hotel.

Walking down the Marine Parade, he fell into a highly technical conversation with Lord Marle concerning certain disreputable persons known to both of them, certain esoteric instruments of navigation and a great many details of this nature that would, indeed, have sadly bored anyone not interested in nautical activity, and it was only when the gentlemen reached the corner of the Strand and Duke of York Street, and Lord Marle gently reminded his companion of his mission, that Mr. Hartley sought to engage the vehicle.

"Have but a little patience, old man, and I think we may contrive to see this situation resolved itself happily," Marle said in parting, and jauntily swung his walking stick in a broad arc.

Mr. Hartley nodded absently, wondering what Marle meant.

Summoned from belowstairs by the sound of the knocker falling upon the lion's head, Russet gave an adjusting twitch to his livery and composed his face into his professional mask of stoic hauteur, a shift from the red-faced and white-lipped expression witnessed by interested parties belowstairs during a set-to with Mr. Russet's autocratic chef, who, upon being informed that he had one hour to prepare a picnic luncheon for four, first threatened the majordomo, then himself with physical violence involving a rending knife. That there may have been storm warnings of such a confrontation brewing ever since Senhora Maria Auglier had put in her fascinating appearance in the hall was a well-known fact, and even Partridge, Sophia's insufferably haughty dresser, neglected her duties in order to witness this most interesting spectacle.

But the footman bringing himself up in Russet's

wake bearing a straw basket packed with such exquisite delicacies as *pâté Fauchon, boeuf froid au poivre, étoiles framboises fromage, and gâteaux au chocolat*—fit only for pigs, Alphonse had wailed, upon such short note—had reason to believe that the dark-eyed Maria's affections had been engaged more by the handsome turn of Lady Denham's coachman's calves than either of her admirers within the hall. He had not been long in service, but he knew when to stow his gab, and merely stood to one side as Russet majestically opened the door to admit the Young Ladies' beaux. The footman was Kentish by birth and did not hold with dark, foreign females of decidedly Latin passions.

Sophia, her hair in curl papers and the hands of her hairdresser still appended to her by a pair of curling tongs, was giving her young relations several last-minute pieces of advice upon the ill effects of too much sun upon the complexion, as they were descending the landing. Yes, they had their parasols, and their Lotion of the Ladies of Denmark, they were assuring her, tying bonnet ribands beneath their chins and turning down an errant flounce. Yes, they would be back before darkfall, and no, they would not comport themselves in Brinshore in such a manner as was likely to bring on sunstroke, highwaymen or disgrace upon the houses of Rockhall and Brandywine.

Mr. Russet was just then pressing a tender bottle of sherry into Lord Marle's hands and begging him to allow it to breathe before serving it with all the certainty that no gentleman knew how to serve wine, and that alfresco eating was not only a most uncivilized method of consumption, but also dangerous, unhealthy and very likely to result in the most dire consequences resultant upon the inexperience of the Quality in trying to feed themselves unassisted.

Lord Marle, who was perfectly capable of preparing

and serving up a hearty, if not gourmet, dinner in a galley during a raging tropical storm solemnly promised that all would be done as Russet instructed and considerably mollified that gentleman by a discreet exchange of currency to be distributed among Sophia's kitchen staff.

"Hullo," he said as the ladies made their descent. Emily, who had not thought to bring a riding habit to Sanditon, was very prettily dressed in a carriage costume suitable to a summer outing. With only a very little assistance from Miranda's vast store of trunks and bandboxes and portmanteaux, she presented herself in a leghorn hat trimmed with pink roses and ribands that tied most becomingly beneath one ear. Over a ruffled walking dress of sprigged muslin, trimmed with convent lace, she wore a spencer of dusty rose linen fastened with tiny mother-of-pearl buttons. Upon her feet, jean half boots of a very charming shade of blue proclaimed her intentions to walk, and under one arm she carried her sunshade and her watercolor kit. In anticipation of an outing of precisely the sort she liked, even her awe of Lord Marle could not prevent a happy glow from suffusing her cheeks, and she was actually able to smile at his compliment. But even more gratifying for her was the manner in which Charles simply stared at her, admiration written large about his handsome face and reflecting deep in the depthless pools of his blue eyes.

Miranda had chosen a riding habit of her favorite dusty mauve, rather dashingly tight to her small form and trimmed in the most Viennese fashion with darker purple cords of silk, fastened from its high collar to its newly styled lowered waist with gold buttons caught in frogs of the same purple cord. Upon her dark curls she had placed a yellow toque from which two very smart plumes curled round her cheek, and upon her hands and feet were gloves and boots of yellow York-shire leather.

The party proceeded to the curb, where a gig and two horses were being maintained by a grizzled man Marle carelessly allowed the ladies to know was Far-thing, his man of all work. To Miranda's sharp eye, this person looked as if he would be more at home upon the rolling deck of a pirate ship than in the saddle, but she could find no fault with the way in which he managed the two horses Marle had chosen to bring with him.

"Your mount, Miss Brandywine, is the white mare," Marle told her as the footman loaded the baskets into the gig and Farthing and Charles assisted Emily in her ascent into this vehicle.

Miranda cast an eye over the white mare, skittishly dancing over the cobbles and smiled at herself. The animal was spirited to a fault, and certainly no mount for an inexperienced horsewoman like her cousin. A handful, in fact, she calculated, and likely to shy at the slightest distraction. She had the uneasy intuition that even Marle could not be such an unspeakable dastard as to select this horse for Emily to ride, and guessed, quite accurately, that there had been a last minute substitution at the livery stable that was meant to pun-ish her a little for her forwardness. But Marle had misjudged his woman, she thought, if he thought that she could be so easily overthrown by a skittish mare.

Out of the corner of her eye, she saw him watching her with that peculiar ironic glint in his smile; there was the subtlest hint of challenge there, she thought.

The animal Marle had chosen for himself was no shag beast either, Miranda thought, an enormous bay gelding that would take more strength than skill to handle.

She walked about the mare, petting her trembling flanks and speaking in a low voice to her, using the old

Gypsy horse language she had learned in Spain. The mare calmed somewhat beneath her touch, but still danced skittishly on her little hooves like a young girl at a dance.

"Throw me up, Marle," Miss Brandywine commanded, and with a sarcastic bow, the viscount did so.

Mounted, Miranda found that she would have some difficulty controlling the mare—the beast definitely had ideas of her own, but with the self-control that Sir Francis had drilled into his daughter in her earliest years, using leg and hand, she was able to put the horse through her paces without betraying any *angst*. "You want a good gallop," she told the mare in Gitane, and stroked her neck comfortingly.

Farthing, having arranged Mr. Hartley, Miss Rockhall, the picnic basket and the wine into the gig to his satisfaction, swung himself into the trap saddle of his own mount, and crossed his arms.

Marle swung himself easily into the saddle and raised his hat to Miranda. "Shall we off?"

She nodded, tight lipped and white knuckled as the mare started to rear, and was aware that Marle had seen her awkwardly sawing the reins.

In this manner the little procession moved down Marine Parade.

"Is it not the most glorious summer day!" Mr. Hartley rhapsodized. "I believed I missed an English June more than any other thing when I was in Vienna." He turned the leathers in his hands and the amiable pair moved at a reasonable pace over the cobbles.

Emily raised her sunshade and murmured some response, studying Charles' delicate profile out of the corner of her eye. An unbidden blush rose to her milky cheeks that matched the unbidden and unfamiliar feelings that were rising in her head. She was a gently reared young lady, and beyond some abrupt and rather distastefully delivered allusions to the mysteries of womanhood and reproduction once alluded to by Lady Rockhall and swiftly dismissed as a necessary informational duty as A Mother, Emily knew very little about the peculiar particulars of love and intimacy. She had been brought up to do her duty by Marrying Well, of course, but were those feelings which rose unbidden and almost frighteningly pleasurable so exactly like those in which the heroines of her favorite novels always seemed to find themselves caught? It was an uneasy thought, and she put it aside, with a great deal of firmness. Mr. Hartley was, after all, Miranda's intended, and as such, completely ineligible.

She realized that he had spoken to her twice, and with a little shake of her head, managed to make some response to his commonplace remarks that would not betray her own feelings.

The day was indeed a beautiful one. All about them, the fields were yellow green with crops pushing their way up from the soil and into the sunlight. Trees hung lush with verdant leaves, and along the hedgerows, wildflowers bloomed in richly colored profusion, twining among the low stone fences and budding shrubbery that framed the rutted old post road. Over the crests of the hills, there were sometimes glimpses of the sea, shimmering an azure blue.

Beneath her, Miranda felt the white mare's muscles straining against her commands. She was an expert horsewoman, having been brought up in the saddle even as she had begun to walk, and had handled animals far beyond the capacities of most females. But she was a small woman, and the mare was large, and, she began to realize, not well broken to saddle.

A thrush, startled out of a thicket, flew across the mare's path, and with a shrieking bray, the animal reared back on its tail, ears flattened, eyes rolling.

Miranda sawed on the leathers with a muttered curse, but the animal had panicked beyond her control. She fought mightily, with all of her skill and strength, but the mare was oblivious to anything but her own panic, and with a buck, she broke into a gallop, heading blindly away from the road, through a break in the hedgerow and across the field.

Miranda was aware, in some part of her consciousness, of Marle's face, white and tense, as he tried to bring his big bay up against the mare, leaning out of the saddle, his hand falling fractions of an inch short of clutching the mare's bridle. Clearly, what he had meant as a joke had turned ugly in a way he had not anticipated, as the mare bore her away, trampling in long strides across the raw earth of the green growing fields, leaving Marle's heavier animal behind.

"Farthing!" the viscount shouted over his shoulder, watching as Miranda's gay yellow cap flew away from her dark curls and rolled into the mud beneath his horse's hooves, the plumes broken and pressed into the mud. He dug his heels into the bay's flanks, cursing beneath his breath as Miranda's purplish habit grew distant.

Without panicking, Miranda was herself cursing, not the mare, but the wretched custom which demanded women be encumbered by skirts and awkward side-saddles. She had been taught to give a runaway horse as much of its own head as possible, in the hopes that it would eventually exhaust itself into some semblance of docility, but as the mare made for a low-hanging tree branch and she slid one foot from the stirrup to lower herself to the level of the horse's back, she realized that she was dealing with another sort of beast entirely. She was dimly aware of clawish branches through her hair and scratching at her face. Without pausing, the mare cleared a low ditch and continued her headlong panic through a field of low corn.

Miranda had relinquished all pretense of control; staying mounted, she realized, was the most important thing; to be thrown might result in something worse than a broken leg or arm on this obstacle course of ditches, stone walls and wooden fences.

Somewhere behind her, she was dimly aware of Marle and Farthing calling encouragement, and she almost laughed as she passed a plowboy, his ox under tethers about his neck, staring openmouthed at the sight of a woman in a purple habit mounted astride upon a runaway white horse.

The mare charged into a thicket, and Miranda pressed her legs into the pounding flanks, feeling sharp thorns tearing through her linen skirts, ripping away her lisle stockings. But she kept her seat, and kept her grip, remembering a hundred other times when she had ridden over muddy battlefields with the dead and dying at her feet and bullets singing over her head. She kept her courage.

"By God," Marle said, watching her. "But she has nerve." There was a grudging hint of admiration in his voice.

Slowly and inexorably, Marle and Farthing gained upon the mare, each one taking a flank in an effort to halt the animal's wild progress.

Miranda was aware of them, but she dared not turn her head to the left or the right for fear of throwing the least weight against her fragile balance.

The wind whistled in her ears; almost absurdly, she was aware of the sound of the sea, just over the hills and through the pine trees. Without looking, she sensed the horses drawing up on either side of her, heard the voices, if not the words of the riders shouting advice; out of the corner of her eye, she was aware, also, of the blur of Marle's body as he swung over in his saddle, his arm reaching out for the mare's bridle.

With her last burst of speed, the mare suddenly broke ahead of her unwanted escort, surging forward toward a trestle fence that loomed unexpectedly up from the rise of a slope. Miranda was unprepared for the jump, and as the mare tensed and strained toward the fence, she felt her balance slipping. Frantically, she tried to right herself, but her legs were tangled in her skirts, and she knew her best chance lay in trying for an easy fall. Slipping her fingers out of the reins, she cradled her head in her arms and rolled away, curling herself, as best she could, into a sort of ball, praying she could avoid the mare's flying hooves and the wooden planks of the fence. The purple habit, flying like a tattered banner on a battlefield, turned in an arc, then dropped into the muddy field just as the mare cleared the fence.

Coming up hard behind, Marle watched as the purple linen rolled across the slope, then lay motionless.

"Get that damned horse!" he cried to Farthing, swinging himself out of the saddle and running toward Miranda.

He knelt by her side, examining her prone form for blood and broken bones, knowing that if she were seriously injured, to move her could be dangerous.

She lay on her side, her face pale and still, her eyes closed. Gently, he pressed his fingers against the side of her neck and found, to his relief, that she had a pulse. As far as he was able to find, she had no broken bones, but as he tenderly probed her arms and legs, Marle cursed himself for the greatest fool in Christendom.

He was just rolling his coat beneath her head when her lashes flickered and her lips parted slightly. From a great distance away, he heard her voice coming in painful gasps. "One must not gallop *ventre à terre*," she mumbled. "It simply is not done in England." A weak smile crossed her face, and she winced as he propped up her head.

"Mir—Miss Brandywine, can you hear me?" Marle inquired, "Are you hurt?"

Miranda's head moved from side to side. "All over," she said faintly. "But I cannot—ah!" She closed her eyes again.

Marle looked about. The plowboy had left his oxen and was running across the furrows toward them, his heavy smock catching the wind, his red face openly curious and concerned.

"Is she daid?" he called breathlessly.

Marle shook his head. "I think, merely, that she has had the wind knocked out of her. Is there a house or an inn nearby—and a doctor?"

The boy drew abreast, looking down at Miranda. "They's the Keg and Anchor, just over t'hill, and Dr. Prescott lives to the village—" he began, but Marle was already assessing his bearings.

"The Keg and Anchor," he said bitterly. "What bloody well else?"

He looked down at Miranda again. She was breathing heavily, her eyes flickering without seeing. She made a little moaning sound in the back of her throat.

"Miss Brandywine, will you allow me to move you? Does your back hurt? Can you feel all your limbs?"

She made a little sound that he took to be an assent, and with the assistance of the awestruck plowboy, managed to mount his horse and scoop her into his arms. She was as light as a kitten, and her face, deprived of its usual animation, was oddly childlike.

Pausing only to instruct the plowboy to send Farthing and the horses on to the Keg and Anchor, and bestowing the rustic lad with a sliver boy, Marle began to head down the slope toward the sea road that led to the Keg and Anchor, managing his mount as gently as he could, lest he further injure his tender burden.

Miranda flung an arm about his neck and lay her cheek against the bosom of his shirt, grimacing slightly "Charles?" she asked distantly.

"Marle," he corrected her.

Miranda sighed and closed her eyes again. "Good. Charles is so *inadequate* in emergencies," she murmured, and lost consciousness with a sigh that under other circumstances, Marle might have taken for contentment.

CHAPTER TEN

The afternoon sun was slanting through the windows in the front parlor when the viscount descended the stairs with an acerbic-looking gentleman whose somber old-fashioned dress and leather bag proclaimed his profession to be medicine. Marle had not recovered his coat, and his shirt, stained and muddied, gave him the appearance of one of the nocturnal habitués of the inn. He looked grim.

Miss Rockhall and Mr. Hartley were seated upon the little settee in the private parlor where Marle had first encountered Miranda. At some point in the afternoon, they had been joined by none other than Mr. Jem Hawkes, and as Marle followed Dr. Prescott into the room, he noted that Jem had been regaling the company with tales of his chosen profession.

"—of course, them Hawkhursts was all a bad lot. But old Thomas Kemp, who was turned off at Tyburn, must be fifty or sixty years ago, he were the worst of a bad bunch. Land smugglers, you see, are a lower class of folk than sea smugglers, that's what I say—"

Emily, seeing Marle and the doctor, rose from the settee, her hands clasped together. "How—?" she asked.

Dr. Prescott used one long finger to push his spectacles up on the bridge of his nose again. "You're the cousin? You ought to go up to her. Mrs. Everley's Susan is sitting with her, but she's been asking for you. A bit banged about and bruised, a sprained wrist and a few pulled muscles, but I think she's had more of a bad fright than anything else. Idea of lettin' a female—or anyone—ride a half-broken horse—" He threw a sharp glance at Marle, then continued. "However, she's a good little horsewoman, and from what his lordship tells me, she knows how to take a fall."

"There," Charles said equably to Emily, "I told you Miranda is capable of anything. Pluck to the backbone, no need to worry. I am Miss Brandywine's fiancé, doctor. Does she wish to see me?"

"Not that I know of. Asked for her cousin," Dr. Prescott replied briefly. He pulled a large gold watch from his pocket and glared at it before snapping the case shut. "I've got a baby over in St. Murda's coming on. Now, my lord, do you remember the laudanum drops, and no moving her for at least a day, recall."

Marle nodded grimly, and followed the doctor to the doorway. When he returned, he threw himself down upon the settee that Emily had vacated and stared moodily into the fire.

"Daresay you ought to call me out, Hartley, after pulling such a stunt as that," he said moodily. "I only though to teach her a lesson—how was I to know that mare was only half-broken?"

Charles stretched his angular frame and threw one leg across the other. "Miss Brandwine is the most capable horsewoman I have ever seen," he said simply.

"She is what I believe they call a neck or nothing rider! Never have I known her to take a fall! I am at a loss to explain it at all. But," he continued with his usual sunny optimism, "I am certain that she will be right as a trivet. She's probably more embarrassed than hurt. Miranda does not like situations she cannot control, you know."

Marle pushed a hand through his hair. "Still and all, Hartley, she took a bad fall, and it was my fault! I never should have mounted her on that beast! God, you ought to call me out! I deserve it."

Mr. Hartley pondered this remarkable statement for a few moments. "Couldn't call you out, Marle. You're my friend. Besides, Miranda wouldn't like it. Don't like getting her into a passion—she can be damned difficult, and I am a peaceable man. Miranda in a temper distracts me from my work. More than likely she'll call you out herself. Challenged some Prussian fellow to a duel in Vienna. Scandal for a day, but it blew over." He shrugged. "That's just Miranda."

Marle projected himself to his feet with a great deal of force. "You're speaking of the woman you intend to marry, for God's sake, Hartley!" he exclaimed in astounded accents. "Have you no intention of protecting her honor?"

Charles blinked. "Oh, Miranda always manages those sorts of things. Miranda is a very managing woman," he added thoughtfully. "Don't worry about her like that at all. Takes me away from my work. She takes care of those things."

Marle stared at Charles for a moment in disbelief, then shook his head. "I don't understand you at all, sometimes, Hartley. How you ever became engaged to that forward, headstrong girl—"

Mr. Hartley pushed his hands into his pockets and regarded his friend from the depths of his pale eyes.

"For that matter, I don't quite understand why you offered for Miss Rockhall, old man. Not in your line at all!"

Marle, having been pressed as far as his temper could take without violent catharsis, stumped out of the room, calling for Farthing.

Jem Hawkes who had been watching all this from his corner, struck a firewheel to his clay pipe. "A right proper mess for certain. Always is whenever you get a woman involved," he added philosophically, picking up his tankard. "Fill you again?"

Mr. Hartley shook his head and closed his eyes. "There is nothing for me to do except wait until I can be of some use. Even my muse has deserted me."

Mr. Hawkes scraped his bootheels on the grate. "Always the same whenever you get skirts into it," he sighed.

Emily found Miranda, pale but bright eyed, almost lost in one of her landlady's plain linsey nightdresses, propped up in an enormous goose down bed under a great many hand-stitched quilts. A young maid was sitting by the bed regarding her anxiously, but the laudanum seemed to be taking its effects, for her eyes were slowly drooping, and she exhibited none of her usual restlessness.

"Emily," she said vaguely upon seeing her cousin. She raised one hand from the bed, and it seemed to drop of its own accord.

"Miranda, my love. You gave us such a fright!" Emily said, casting herself across the counterpane, brushing the tangled curls from Miranda's damp forehead. "Are you really quite all right?"

Miranda smiled and nodded. "Just a bit embarrassed. To think that *I* could not handle a horse! Lord, I am so *mortified*, Emmie, for letting that mare bolt with me...poor Marle...he wanted to teach me a lesson, and it backfired upon him, just like Wyngate's rockets...." She managed a thin little laugh. "Emily, who is worse, he or I? Or both of us?"

"Now please do not tease yourself with such silly things," Emily said. "I am here to take care of you, and you will be all right, the doctor says...of course—"

"Ruined our day..." Miranda murmured. "Charles and Emily—not me—Marle?"

"Of course," Emily replied soothingly, holding Miranda's hand until she was certain that her cousin had dropped into an exhausted slumber.

"You looked fagged to death, Miss," the little maid said. "Meaning no disrespect. But Miss is pretty well done in—his lordship set that wrist for her, and stood over Dr. Prescott like he was one of them fancy Lunnon surgeons, makin' sure all was done proper. Mrs. Jenks has put up a nice joint for your dinner, and laid out a basin in the room opposite if you wish to wash up; she says we may not get the Quality here, but she does know how proper ladies should be taken care of and his lordship is by way of being known here, so now, you just take care of yourself. I'll sit with Miss, like his lordship asked. I've got to do with trying to fix Miss's habit so she may wear it again." By way of illustration, she held up the purple gown and a needle and thread.

Miss Rockhall was reluctant to leave her cousin thus, but the maid was firm, and she did find that her sadly frayed nerves were a great deal soothed by towels and clean water. Like Charles, she had come to see Miranda as an indestructible being, capable of almost miraculous recover, and while her delicate nerves were wrought, Mr. Hartley's sublime confidence in her cousin had done much to allay her fears.

Upon descending, she found Lord Marle and Mr. Hartley in the parlor, a thin thread of tension between

165

them only somewhat allayed by the setting of covers and the prospect of a decent supper being served.

But Lord Marle refused any nourishment. "I was going to send Farthing back to inform Lady Rockhall of the day's events and shoot that damned horse—pardon me, Miss Rockhall, this day is not at all what I had intended for you and me, but that shall have to wait for another time! Instead, I shall go back with Farthing in the gig and return the horses to the livery stable, inform your aunt of the day's events and fetch back Miss Braydywine's abigail together with her things. It is late now, and it is entirely likely that I shall not be able to find a suitable conveyance for Miss Brandywine until tomorrow morning at the earliest. Will you be all right with what you have? The good Mrs. Jenks will see to your needs, and has already, I believe, made up two chambers for you."

"I shall sleep on a trundle in Miranda's room," Emily said softly. "In case she needs me during the night. I am not at all a bad nurse, you know. Papa is frequently given to gout, and when he is in such a state, I am the only person who may come near him!"

Marle looked relieved. For an instant, he seized Emily's hand. "Miss Rockhall, I—" he began, then cut himself off as she instinctively shrank from his touch. "Do you but follow the doctor's instructions—she must have a sponge bath when she wakes, and some of that tincture should she grow restless; only beef broth and barley water—and be certain that she does not get set upon one of her fidgets! She must rest still, you know—"

Emily nodded.

"Shouldn't worry about her! Miranda's as tough as a trooper!" Mr. Hartley said, tucking his napkin into his lap and eyeing a rib with some longing.

Marle cast him an odd look and took his leave.

Whatever the irregularities of the Keg and Anchor's

cellars, they did yield up an excellent Burgundy, and laboring, Mrs. Jenks outdid herself. As the young lad who served them blushingly announced, Missus felt that she might not be the equal of the fancified Frenchie cooks on Marine Parade, but that what she did serve was good, wholesome English cooking, and she has not yet received any complaints.

This was amply proved by the repast he laid before Emily and Charles. There was a joint of spring lamb, and a goodly rib of beef, served with light, hot bread fresh from the ovens and covered with good country butter. A light spring salad of new spinach and sprig lettuce done with a sherrry dressing and a dish of stewed compote together with a remove of curried vegetables, and a second bottle of Burgundy from those excellent if very unorthodox cellars.

By the time the covers had been removed with coffee, cheese, fruit and the most delicately wonderful strawberry creams Miss Rockhall had ever tasted, both she and Charles had all but forgotten Miss Brandywine upstairs and Lord Marle upon the road to Sanditon. Miss Rockhall, who had never in her life had above two glasses of champagne at one time, and Mr. Hartley, who after one particularly riotous drinking bout at Cambridge had limited his imbibing severely, were, not to put too blunt a face upon it, more than a trifle foxed.

With the capable little Jean tending Miranda's ponderous slumber abovestairs and the tap filling with the Keg and Anchor's regulars, with all their attendant noise and cheer, it only seemed natural that Mr. Hartley and Miss Rockhall should be entranced into the outside world by the beauties of a warm summer night.

The fingernail of the waning moon hung over the ocean, and the surf rolled across the rocky beachfront in cascades of spray. A fine summer breeze rustled through the pines, and a thousand katydids were singing their songs.

Mr. Hartley and Miss Rockhall walked along the narrow wooden steps which led down to the beach, giggling somewhat incoherently.

At the foot of the stairs, Mr. Hartley thrust his hands into his pockets and looked up at the moon, his poet's soul blazing with inspiration. As he searched his pockets for notepad and pencil, he quite missed the most interesting sight of Miss Rockhall kicking off her jean boots, seating herself upon a rock to strip off her silk stockings, gathering up her skirt about her knees and running—positively *running* in a manner that would have caused her Mama to collapse into a bout of severe hysterics—along the tideline of the beach, her arms outspread, her blond hair falling out of its pins, her long legs splashing with a novel and joyous freedom in the surf.

"Diana, ancient goddess of the moon, Neptune sees thee upon the sea..." Mr. Hartley was muttering to himself, his handwriting scrawling off the page, due, no doubt, to the combination of Burgundy and darkness. "Hm—that isn't quite right. Diana, lunar beauty, married to Neptune of the sea, sees—no. Free Diana—"

Fate and the muses suddenly conspired, and Mr. Hartley looked up at Miss Rockhall wading in the surf.

Quite simply, it was the most beautiful vision he had ever beheld; with her face lifted toward the sliver of light, her long hair blowing gently about her face and her pink muslin dress, dampened from the sea, clinging to her long limbs, Emily Rockhall was transformed from a rather proper (and perhaps a little mundane) English miss into a Divinity.

Heedless of his shoes and breeches, Mr. Hartley

thrust his notebook into his pocket and walked into the surf toward Emily.

As he drew up upon her, Emily looked up at him and smiled rather dizzily. "Char-les," she said happily, "I am a trifle *foxed.*"

"Emily," Mr. Hartley said simply.

"Charles," Miss Rockhall repeated in an entirely different tone of voice.

Their kiss tasted of a rare old, smuggled Burgundy, and that made it all the sweeter for both of them. Being embraced by Mr. Hartley in *such a fashion* was quite different from the chaste peck she had received from Lord Marle upon their engagement, Miss Rockhall discovered much to her pleasure. The vague pronouncement of her governess that "when the time came" she would know all about the mysteries of life suddenly became very, very clear to her, and instead of modestly demurring, she found herself wanting Charles to go much farther.

For a very long while that was also a very short time, they embraced. Mr. Hartley found a whole other infinite universe within the arms of Emily Rockhall. He felt as if he had come home from a very long journey.

"It is not just the wine," he murmured, after a while.

Emily looked up at him from clear eyes. "It is not the wine at all—since that first night I saw you, standing in the garden, I—I have felt this way."

Charles passed a hand over her hair with a sense of wonder. "This sweet madness in my heart—I, too have felt it since that very night when I first saw you standing in the window above me—"

It was some minutes more before either one was able to speak.

As if a chill wind had washed over the warm summer night, Emily lay her head upon Charles' shoulder.

"Miranda. Oh, how can I be such a traitor to my own cousin?"

"She is indeed a goddess—a most marvelous woman, but I have not only betrayed her, I have betrayed Marle! My friend and patron!"

The waves washed gently against the sand.

"I would rather be dead than face marriage with Lord Marle when at last I have found you," Emily said bitterly. "I should cast myself into the sea first!"

A seagull flew overhead with its eerie cry.

"Miranda is an excellent woman. How fortunate I felt that she had singled me out of all her other admirers. It all happened so swiftly—I never expected that we would become betrothed. I knew Sir Francis did not approve of me; I felt my suit to be hopeless, and yet, when she proposed—"

"Miranda proposed?" Despite herself, Emily giggled.

"Well, of course she did. What could I, a penniless secretary, offer her? She and Sir Francis had just had one of their rows about some Prussian with waxed mustaches and—Good Lord, she seemed so distant, so unattainable—she was always surrounded by a host of men—I never thought—Miranda just seemed to sweep away everything that stood in her path...."

"Miranda has been so very good to me....I could never hurt her."

"Marle—Emily, do you realize that he has agreed to finance my experiments with gas-lighting and navigational instruments?"

"He is a most admirable man. So—capable."

"Miranda is capable also."

Far out in the ocean, a buoy tolled mournfully.

"We will be hurting them both so dreadfully—and they are both such admirable people," Charles said without much enthusiasm. "I could never support you in the style to which you have been accustomed. My land in Hampshire is little more than a farm, my house little more than a cottage—I only have three servants, and one is a tenant farmer."

"I can dress a joint, and sew a good seam. I once made Papa a shirt for Christmas. I know several ways of preserving calf's foot jelly and—"

"Lord Marle has vast estates. He is a man of style and fashion. A mansion in London, a yacht, a life to which I could never—"

"Miranda is dashing and fashionable and witty and intelligent, and she knows exactly how to go on in the world. She is the sort of female who any man would be lucky to marry," Emily said doubtfully.

"But it is you I wish to marry, not Miranda. Here in Sanditon, I have seen my feelings for Miranda for what they really are—the flattering attentions of such a female must excite one who has never really been taken very seriously by the world. Miranda persuaded herself that she loved me out of a sense of rebellion from the military life she had been brought up to. I am a man of peace, not war, a man of thought, not action."

"War and action make me very nervous," Emily said. "I do not want to have to be a countess and live in that vast house and always feel like a very small churchmouse. A little house in Hampshire is exactly what I want, Charles."

"Then it is exactly what you will have," he said firmly.

"Oh, Charles," Emily sighed. "If only we could…"

"We shall," Mr. Hartley said manfully. "A man of Marle's character, of his position, must only snap his fingers to find a bride. Miranda has never lacked for suitors. I doubt if either of them shall much pine for us."

"Mama," Emily said in greater tones of terror.

"I shall handle your mother," Mr. Hartley promised rashly. "And I shall handle Marle."

"But after all Miranda has done for me..."

"Miranda will manage. No doubt by now, Sir Francis is ready to make peace with her, and she will return to Vienna and find a hundred men waiting for her—all far more eligible than I!"

"I could never enjoy a moment's happiness under such circumstances, knowing that I have been such an *odious wretch* as to steal my cousin's fiancé, in the most vile act of treachery—" Emily declared, breaking away from Charles' embrace and looking out across the ocean. Miserably, she clamped her hands to her bosom. "This is wrong, wrong, Charles—it is only moon madness and nothing more! We must not!"

Charles pushed a hand through his raven locks. "Miranda is the most admirable of females," he agreed unhappily. "She is beautiful, dashing, gay and—and totally wrong for me, as I am for her! I see it now, and though I wish by all the gods that I did not, that it were otherwise, I have met you, I have known you, and, alas, I have the sweet pain of knowing that I have finally discovered love! Emily!" Charles, in a rare act of assertion, seized Miss Rockhall's shoulders and spun her about to face him. Almost as if hypnotized, she gazed into the depths of his pale blue eyes.

"Tell me at once that you do not love me, Emily, and I shall never see you again! Only tell me that what I feel is not what you are feeling, and I shall be gone from this place and your life forever."

Emily struggled valiantly within herself to turn away, or at least to speak. Her lips parted and closed again, and his eyes held her captive in their depths. "I cannot," she whispered, "Charles, I cannot tell you

172

this. If—if you were to leave—if I were never to see you again, I believe I would die."

"Most beloved," Mr. Hartley breathed passionately, clasping Miss Rockhall's damp form against his breast. "You have made me the happiest man on earth."

"And myself the most wretched female. Oh, Charles, Mama was right—falling in love only leads to the most wretched complications."

Mr. Hartley manfully embraced Miss Rockhall, taking her breath away. With one hand beneath her chin, he brought her face up to his own and smiled bravely. "You are my sun, my moon, all my stars of an infinite universe. Emily, I'd wade through hell for you, and the world be damned. But I shall not bring dishonor upon your head. No! There must be a way to contrive! Even if we must elope to the continent, we *shall* contrive!"

She shook her head. "This world was not made for people like you and me, Charles, we are dreamers and meditators, not people of action...."

"My beloved has such wonderful common sense," he murmured, delighted. "She can dress a joint and sew seams in linen and yet she plays like an angel unawares." He sighed. "All the arguments you present are rational; every obstacle stands in our path to happiness; but Emily, Emily, I would rather live in some Italian garret with you than in that fine London townhouse Miranda plans to build!" His lips brushed lightly across her cheek. "I am erratic, and often forgetful and careless, and go off upon the nackiest of starts, but, my Emily, for all of that, it is you—and *only* you—who would make my life worth living. To continue without you beside me would be meaningless; this I know inside my heart where the deepest truths lie."

"And I am shy, and silly and very, very goosish, but

oh, Charles, I know my heart, really I do...." She shook her head. "I could not bear life without you, either."

"This I do not yet know. If only I could take Marle into my confidence, for he is the most complete man—"

"Miranda could manage, if only—"

"No. No, my love. Dreamers we may be, but we are not moon mad. After six months of marriage to me, Miranda would wish me to the devil, I know, even if she does not yet understand that. Perhaps for a week or so, she will be angry, but her heart is strong, and she has had a hundred suitors, each one more eligible and better suited to her than I. She will come about, I know, as will Marle—and to see you married to Marle, excellent man though he be, I could not bear! I should put a gun to me head!"

"Charles, no!" Emily protested.

With considerable poetic license, he nodded, briefly snagged upon the vision of himself as a Werther; but perhaps Emily's common sense was infectious, for he shook this off and addressed himself to the problem at hand.

"Can you but wait for a little while? When she has recovered, I shall talk to Miranda—she shall see that we will not suit. Already, I think, in her secret heart, she must know how wrong it would be for her to buckle with me...in the past few weeks she and I have seen each other, not through the candlelight of some Viennese ballroom, but as we really are!"

"Lord Marle—"

"Exactly," Mr. Hartley said mysteriously, his face illuminated with some inner thought. "Exactly. Only be patient awhile longer, my love, and all will come to rights."

"I do not see how," Emily said unhappily. "But I believe you. Charles, you *will* contrive."

"Yes," Mr. Hartley promised, although he really had not the vaguest idea of how he might contrive. But intoxicated more by love than wine, he stroked Emily's corn-gold hair tenderly, confident in his eternal belief that something would turn up.

CHAPTER ELEVEN

The sun was streaming through the calico curtains directly upon Emily's face when she finally awoke in the morning. Through the haze of a cotton-wool-stuffed head, she was able to perceive that the morning was far well advanced, and that even a few hours of extra sleep had done little to restore her mind from the night's imbibing. Little by little, the scene that had taken place upon the beach reentered her consciousness, but such were the effects of drinking Burgundy upon her inexperienced system that not even these memories would allow her to open her eyes and acknowledge her awakening. But it must be admitted that some vague reflections upon Mr. Hartley's declarations at first allowed her a measure of comfort against her rebelling body. Only when the gradual realization reached her that nothing had been solved, or resolved, by this new turn, and that indeed, matters were even more hopelessly tangled than ever, did she groan and attempt to rise from her trundle bed.

"Ah, good morning, my love," Miranda greeted her cheerfully from the chair. Lost in a voluminous linsey-woolsey dressing gown from the landlady's wardrobe, with only a few bruises and the beginnings of a rather base-looking plaster on her eyebrow, Miranda seemed, to Emily's wretched eye, far more healthy than anyone who had been through such an ordeal had any right to be. Almost at once, Miss Rockhall was washed by a second sense of guilt against her cousin, and struggled valiantly to pull herself out of bed. "You should not be up, Miranda," she scolded through a dry mouth.

"The doctor was most particular about saying you must rest—" Emily sat upon the edge of her cot and pressed her fingertips into her thundering temples.

"Fudge and nonsense," Miranda replied. "The surgeon we had with us in Spain would have laughed to see me wrapped in cotton wool for such a trivial thing. A night's sleep and all I feel is an acute sense of embarrassment at my own inadeptness!" But as she hobbled for the tea tray upon the table, Emily noted her cousin winced a bit as she placed her slight weight upon her sprained ankle.

"Let me—" Miss Rockhall began, but Miranda waved her away impatiently. "Only sprains and bruises. Once in Portugal, I broke my arm—now there was plain and simple agony, I assure you, for I had to ride nearly five miles in the rain to have it set, and Sir Francis made me bite a bullet between my teeth lest I cry." She poured and stirred, presenting Emily with a teacup. "Drink, you will fell much better if you have some tea and a hot bath, my dear. That must have been quite a head you tied upon yourself last night. Charles should be shamed for allowing you to drink so much."

Emily gratefully sipped at the hot tea, and Miranda hobbled back to the chair again. "Apparently he fears my displeasure—and well he ought, for to allow you to drink a half a bottle of Burgundy—well! Anyways, he has retreated upon us this morning, and where he may be, I have not the faintest idea. He only left a note stating that he would see us in due course. I swear, Charles can be exasperating. But Lord Marle is belowstairs, and we are to have such a treat—we are to be carried back to Sanditon in his yacht!"

"Charles is gone?" Emily said in a small, unhappy voice.

"Left this morning on horseback, I believe. So typical of him, you know. He is full of weird fits and starts, and that, you know, I find excessively annoying. Poets! There is no accounting for their whims, is there? But it don't signify, for I am quite out of sorts with him anyway, for making you so foxed. Now, I won't talk anymore, but you will feel very much more the thing when the girl brings up your bathwater and you have had a good soak. I won't tease you any further, my dear."

Emily nodded miserably, too overcome to speak, or even attempt to elicit further details of Mr. Hartley's disappearance. It was depressingly clear to her that last night's words had all been a bag of moonshine, and Charles, unable to face her upon the day, had thoughtfully and tactfully removed his embarrassing presence from her company.

She felt woefully stung; and worse, she felt as if her heart, so newly awakened, was in dangerous peril of being broken.

While the little chambermaid was carrying copper pots of hot water from the kitchen to Miss Rockhall's tin tub, Miranda managed to array herself in the repaired and somewhat tattered purple habit without feeling too much pain. The opiate had worn off in the night, and she was aware of the stiffness in every muscle in her body, but pride and determination allowed her to descend the stairs unaided, and find Lord Marle seated in the parlor, idly pursuing an ancient copy of a sporting periodical.

Seeing Miss Brandywine, he rose to his feet and crossed the room, holding out both hands, his expression unreadable, as he caught her just before she managed to fall.

An interested witness might have said that Marle held Miss Brandywine for a few seconds longer than was absolutely necessary to support a small lady with a sprained ankle into a chair, but an interested witness might also have noted that Miss Brandywine, for all of her show of mobility, made no demur when she was almost bodily picked up and carried to the comfortable wing chair by the cold hearth.

"Ma'am, have you no sense at all? The doctor has strictly forbidden you to attempt to walk for at least three days!" Marle said harshly, regarding her with that same unreadable expression in his eyes.

Miranda, feeling a steady throb in her foot and ankle, nonetheless waved away this medical advice with one small hand. "It don't fadge," she said. "I've been through far worse—"

"I am sure that you have, ma'am, but even my abject contrition for landing you into such a predicament doesn't warrant my having to hear a tale of how you amputated your own limb in the Pyrenees," he replied.

Miranda shot him a look as unreadable as his own. "When were you ever contrite, Marle? And why should you be, when it was my ham-handedness that landed me in the blue devils?" she asked sharply, settling back into the chair with a little involuntary sigh.

The faintest hint of a smile twitched at his lips, but Marle reprimanded himself and drew down his brows sternly. "I am asking your forgiveness for what I consider to be an unpardonable piece of mischief on my part, Miss Brandywine, and you are throwing my apology back into my face! If you *must* act like a gentleman, at least accept the honors of one!"

Miranda closed her eyes and folded her hands across her waist, elbows propped upon the arms of the chair. "I see no reason why you should feel you need apologize for my mistakes, Marle! Doing it too brown! I have spent half my life on horseback, and Sir Francis would be the first to say that I botched it badly! Should have given the mare her head in the first place. No need to waste your manners upon me, when you might have used them to advantage upon your fiancée, sir!" Her eyes opened to little slits. "But I forget—you have no manners, as you are forever telling me."

"If you so much as move a muscle from that chair, Miss Brandywine, I will—"

"You'll what, Lord Marle?" Miranda asked sweetly.

"Never mind what I'll do. Is Emily making ready?"

"Yes. She and Charles broke a bottle of Burgundy between them last night; I fear she is not at all the thing this morning."

"Females!" Lord Marle exclaimed, striding out of the room. When she was certain he was gone, Miranda gingerly rubbed her swollen wrist.

"If Charles were here—" she began to say, and then settled back, realizing that if Charles were there, Marle would do exactly the same thing.

"Men," she said in tones of loathing, and stretched out her leg, propping her sore foot upon the grate.

A hearty breakfast of eggs, kidneys, sausage and muffins did much to make what fractional improvements were possible in Miranda's foul temper, and if she did note the listless way in which Emily picked at her toast, or the manner in which Marle rather imperiously hurried the ladies through their repast, she was far too hazy and aching to pay it much note.

Lord Marle's *Sea Wind*, however, did pluck up her interests somewhat, and the novelty of being swung aboard from the tender to the yacht in a bosun's chair, and encouraging Emily not to be afraid of this rather precarious device, put her a little more in charity with the viscount.

Seated in a chair upon the afterdeck with a blanket wrapped about her legs, she was able to cast an eye over the vessel and mourn that she was not permitted to go below, as Emily was, to rest during the short voyage to Sanditon. With interest, she watched Marle direct his crew, and even managed a cordial greeting for Farthing, who skippered the vessel.

For his part, Marle extended Miranda the courtesy of his company, and was somewhat pleased to note that Miss Brandywine was not totally without marine experience. She was able to comment favorably upon the rake of his masts and the particularly elegant style of his scribing, sympathize with his difficulties in ordering the precise sort of Manila hemp he wished for his rigging from the boatyard in Sanditon, and eventually pronounced the ketch to be *yar,* a term which delighted Lord Marle far more than Miss Brandywine thought necessary.

Nonetheless, it was a fine day, and she enjoyed the feel of the boat moving under sail, cutting through the blue coastal waters far more than she might have expected. If Lord Marle tended upon the joys and peculiarities of sailing his ketch in terms far more esoteric than those at her immediate command, she was at least able to listen with the look, if not the reality, of comprehension, and nod sagely here and there to indicate

181

that she was listening. Miss Brandywine's pride would not allow her to admit that she was a far less experienced sailor than Lord Marle had been led to believe by her narrow glossary of nautical terms, but she so enjoyed the novelty of seeing him completely relaxed and totally at his ease in his own environment that she felt compensated for the pity she was feeling for poor Emily confined belowdecks with Maria in the worst sort of *mal de mer*.

"This is more like," she said upon one occasion. "I should like to do this for the rest of my life!"

Marle was astounded by his own reaction to Miss Brandywine's interest; surely her approval or disapproval of his ketch could mean very little to *him*, but his mood increased to such a degree that he was able to order his steward to break out a bottle of some excellent (and smuggled) sherry for himself and Miss Brandywine.

Stripped of his coat, his shirt open to expose his powerful neck, his arms exposed to the sun as he rolled up his sleeves and took the helm, it did seem to Miss Brandywine that Lord Marle was a very different person. In her brief experiences with private sailing vessels, most men tended to take on the personality of the regrettable Captain Bligh the minute their feet were placed upon a rolling deck. Even Charles, the mildest of gentlemen in general, had shown a most unhappy tendency to incite his crew of one to mutiny in a row about the river one fine day. But here, while it was always certain that Marle was in command of his crew, there was none of that dreadful masculine arrogance she had come to expect. His orders were given clearly and sharply, and the crew fell to with a precision and competence that she had only seen from men who respect their leader's command; she was not surprised to learn that the *Sea Wind* had won several races with other yachts.

Rather dreamily, she sipped at her sherry and thought about what it must be like to cruise all the exotic places of the world, places of which she had only read in books, Scandinavia's fjords, America, the West Indies, Brazil, Nova Scotia, the islands of the South Pacific where cannibals and headhunters roamed the jungle—*there* would be adventure! she thought pleasantly. What a little fool Emily was, to quake at a few rough seas, poor dear Emily, not that she meant that for a moment, but it was beyond her comprehension that anyone would wish to stay in one place, when there was all the world out there, waiting to be experienced and explored....

Almost as if he had caught her thoughts, Marle turned from the wheel and smiled at her.

She smiled back, almost forgetting that she was out of sorts with the viscount.

"Yar," he said again, and laughed.

It was just upon five o'clock when Marle deposited a neurasthenic Miss Rockhall and a Miss Brandywine only slightly worse for the wear and tear upon the bosom of the Dowager. Lady Rockhall, neck-deep in party plans and inured to escapades of all sorts, having dealt with everything from skinned knees to influenza over the years of childrearing, received them in the same spirit in which they were delivered and sent them both immediately to their beds for barley water and beef broth, with strict instructions that they were not to leave their rooms until breakfast time.

"Very pretty, Marle," she siad to the viscount. "Exactly the sort of thing one would *expect* from one of Mad Jack Runford's brats!"

Feeling very much like a castigated schoolboy, Marle again apologized and took his leave, having been abjured several times before he was allowed to escape from Sophia's presence not to forget that he was to present himself at Number Four no later than eight-thirty on Friday evening for his fiancée's rout party.

By the time his purposeful walk had brought him to the portals of the Sanditon Hotel, however, he was very much himself again. A scrawled note informing Lady Denham that she need not expect him for dinner was dispatched with Farthing to the Place, and Marle, pausing only before the vast mirror in the lobby to adjust his perfect cravat, betook himself up the stairs.

A knock upon Mr. Hartley's door produced a response to the effect that a maid need not turn down the bed, but the viscount entered anyway.

Lord Marle, in his brief association with Mr. Hartley's mode of living, had grown somewhat inured to the erratic manner in which his poetic friend dwelt amid crumpled papers, strewn wardrobe and bits and pieces of his various inventor's models dropped wherever they chanced to land, but even Marle felt that the state of Mr. Hartley's chambers was, this evening, rather a bit much. The viscount was not overly given to considering the feelings of servants, but as he glanced about the small room, he did feel a certain sympathy for the chambermaid whose job it was to create order and tidiness from this maelstrom.

Most of Charles' wardrobe seemed to be scattered about the bed and the floor rather than folded neatly in the empty clothes-press which stood against one wall—no, not quite empty, for it was being used to store boxes of wire and metal, the raw materials of his current brainchild—the bed was unmade and strewn with books, old newspapers and crumpled sheets which betrayed Mr. Hartley's muse's holiday from her poet. A towel lay across the washstand over the upended ewer, and the commode looked as if Mr. Hartley had been using its surface as a writing desk, while the window curtains had been thrown back and held with unmatching stockings to admit the seaside light.

Mr. Hartley himself was seated at the desk before the window in his shirt-sleeves, his cravat hanging loosely about his neck, his shirt opened to his clavicle, his shoestrings undone and his head buried in his hands, the very picture of poetic block and despair.

Rising from the rubble accumulated upon the surface of the desk, there stood a magnificent brass box, whose purpose was as mysterious as the luster it gave off in the half twilight of the room.

"What, Hartley, stuck?" the viscount asked casually, laying his hat and cane gingerly upon the laundry on the chair.

At the sound of Marle's voice, Mr. Hartley's form snapped out of the chair as if a spring had been released. In what Marle could only consider the worst stance from, Charles put up his fists and glared at the viscount through black-rimmed eyes. "Marle! If you have come to demand satisfaction, sir, than name your sec—"

His lordship regarded Mr. Hartley quizzically. There were heavy circles beneath his blue and rather bloodshot eyes, and his jaw was black with the need of a shaving. "Shot your bolt, Hartley? Not feeling all the thing?" Marle inquired mildly.

"There is nothing you can do! Nothing! Our minds are made up!" Charles repeated. "I'll move heaven and earth if I must, but I will not and cannot—"

"Burgundy will do that to you. Very bad to be a three-bottle man. Unless you've taken up opium smoking—understand that's fashionable among poets these days. Rotten stuff, opium." Marle looked about the room for evidence of a bottle or a pipe, but could only see a plate with the remains of a day-old slice of cheese and a half-eaten apple.

Mr. Hartley's fists wavered, and he sank slowly back into his chair, burying his face in his hands again. "It's no drink—or no drug, Marle! It's no illness of the body, but an illness of the emotions!"

Flipping up his coattails, Lord Marle perched uneasily upon the edge of the unmade bed, regarding Mr. Hartley's despair with interest. "When you're in one of those poetical moods of yours, Hartley, I despair of your sanity. Can't you talk like a normal man? Swallowed a spider?"

Mr. Hartley lifted his handsome face from his hands and turned his profile from side to side. "No, I am quite in funds, thanks to you—which makes my sins even more unforgivable!"

"Well, genius takes its own time, old man," Marle reassured him. "I only stopped by you know, to have a look at our invention's progress and to tell you that I'd brought the ladies safely back to Marine Parade."

This set Charles off even further. "The ladies! God, Marle, I am a wretched man! I should be the happiest, most blessed man on the face of the earth, and yet circumstances have forced me to contemplate putting a shell through my brain! Far, far better if I were dead than to have trapped the most innocent, gentle creature in nature into the hopeless confines of my doomed love!" Charles cried, pushing his hands through his hair.

Several thoughts passed through the viscount's mind. First, he ascertained that Mr. Hartley had no weapon to hand, secondly, that Miss Brandywine was hardly the sort of female one could call an innocent, gentle creature; the third thought caused his expression to take on that unreadable cast, and with a short, hidden smile, he shook his head lightly from side to side, rising from the bed, to clap Mr. Hartley's shoulder.

"What you need, Charles, is a decent sort of supper, and a good bottle of wine. Food will make you feel much better, you know, and then over a good piece of beef, we may talk it out. Come, let me valet you—you must have a clean shirt somewhere in this pile, but, my dear Hartley, these cravats will never do, poet or nay!"

"Too good! Too good!" Mr. Hartley said feveredly. "Marle—Vincent, I cannot break bread with you, not after what I have done!"

"Charles, will you stop playing the fool and sit down?" Lord Marle asked, stropping Mr. Hartley's razor. "We will talk—a most long and civilized talk, I promise you—over a bottle of good port and some fine Cubaño cigars, and after dinner! Nothing spoils my digestion more than flights of poetry and overnice feeling with my roast beef!"

Lord Marle was an excellent valet, but even he could not be expected to work miracles with the raw material provided by Mr. Hartley's diminished wardrobe; between outfitting his friend and calming his mysterious, if periodical, outbursts of agony, Marle was feeling quite ready for his own supper, and certain that despite Mr. Hartley's protests that he could not touch a bite, was fairly certain that his friend would be tempted by the excellent bill of fare offered in the hotel's dining room.

The two gentlemen were just descending the staircase and making for that room when Marle, glancing toward the desk, froze in his tracks.

"Good Lord," he breathed, pressing himself backwards into an alcove that displayed a statue of Diana.

Mr. Hartley, unwrapping himself from his own preoccupations long enough to follow his lordship's glance, saw a rather sour-faced female in a green baize bonnet remonstrating with the clerk about the rates in a rather too cultivated voice while her abigail rather fruitlessly tried to pile up the steadily accumulating collection of luggage.

"Not quite in your style, Marle," Mr. Hartley said absently. "Never knew you to flirt with mutton dressed as lamb."

And indeed, the poet's instinct was upon target, for the lady remonstrating with the clerk, the manager and the maître d'hôtel was attired in the pastel muslins and ribands of the first season debutante, making a rather incongruous appearance against the matron her face and figure betrayed her to be.

"Damn your eyes, Hartley, she ain't one of my flirts! That is Lady Rockhall, Emily's mother, and a more mushrooming, toad-eating female you will never find than that tartar! Merry hell, don't let her see us, or we'll never be shed of her for the rest of the evening! I'll wager I know what mischief brought that dragon into Sanditon just when things were going along so well, but you may rest assured that she hasn't yet shown her face at Marine Parade!"

Mr. Hartley, staring with an awful fascination at the bane of his beloved's existence, barely heard his companion's comments.

"Quick, Hartley, into the dining room! I will not have my meal spoiled by Lady Rockhall—or any other female—until we have eaten a good beef and settled our digestions with a bottle of fine old smuggled port."

CHAPTER TWELVE

All that morning, a steady stream of tradesmen had been arriving at Number Four. Oysters in their wicker baskets, still dripping with sea water, jostled with florists' boys bearing armloads of freshly cut roses, while the butcher's cart nearly took a wheel off the vintner's dray.

The notable Alphonse had twice threatened to give his notice and once threatened the scullery maid with being boiled alive along with the lobsters, while Sophia's dresser had descended belowstairs with an armload of dresses, in a state bordering upon the frenzied, and had to be treated with smelling salts and a glass of the Best from my lady's cellars in order to continue her duties. Just as it seemed that this crisis was about to be avoided, Miss Brandywine's Maria appeared upon the scene, and these two ladies immediately commenced a bilingual contretemps that drew even Alphonse away from his own problems to witness, freely giving encouragement to both sides.

Russet, majestic despite a baize apron over his vestment, had no sooner managed to settle this dispute than he was called upon to assist two footmen in lowering the huge crystal chandelier from its moorings in the ballroom. This being no easy job in itself, his immediate supervision was needed for every step of the process in which it was lowered upon its block and tackle and had each delicate prism gently washed by several underlings until it sparkled. All about the small ballroom, an army of workmen were busily engaged in hanging bowers of roses from wicker trellises fitting thousands of candles into their sockets, removing the chairs from their holland covers, waxing the parquet floor, setting up the orchestra dais, unsealing French windows closed for two years and setting up the long tables from which Lady Rockhall's guests would procure champagne, wine and all manner of delicate refreshment. The orchestra leader and his satellites were in attendance, conveying their stands and instruments into the room.

Maids and footmen moved up and down the stairs, bearing piles of linen and freshly polished silver trays; delicate crystal glasses chimed as they narrowly avoided a collision with an enormous épergne coming the other way. From the attics to the cellars, Number Four was a buzzing hive of activity, and Russet, fancied, looking about himself with a truly professional sense of satisfaction, all was moving according to plan. In thirty years of service, he trusted he had learned how to manage an entertainment; and as Lady Rockhall's deputy upon earth, he considered it his prime duty to relieve that lady of everything but the chosing of her guests, gowns and jewels. If left to her own devices, Lady Rockhall would have made a muddle of it, anyway, he wisely understood, and while allowing her to believe that she was in supreme command, he knew that it was his own expertise that gave his employer her renown as a hostess. That she paid him a handsome yearly sum for just such services as this did not at all awe him; Russet knew himself to be worth every penny of his princely remuneration. And like the Diety in his Heaven, with all right with the world (as the poet said), he masterfully orchestrated all that he surveyed with the smoothness of a well-functioning clock.

He was, as a matter of fact, in the process of adjusting the grand timepiece upon the landing to match his own watch when a footman approached him with a woebegone look.

Russet closed the casing with a neat snap and placed his own timepiece into its accustomed pocket.

"Well, Garvey? Has one of the maids broken a prism, or is Alphonse threatening the poulterer with a *béarnaise* sauce on his wig?" he asked mildly.

"It's neither of those, sir," the young man gasped. "It's Miss Emily's Ma upon the doorstep, sir! I seen her as I were apolishing the windows."

"Lady Rockhall," Russet said in tones of stunned disbelief.

"The very same, sir. She'll be pulling the bell at any second, sir," the footman added somewhat breathlessly.

Russet squared his shoulders and removed his apron. Placing it in the hands of the footman, he proceeded down the steps with a magnificent tread, reaching the door just as the first peal had rung out.

Whatever his thoughts, his face was an impassive mask as he threw open the portals to behold the present baroness, attired in lavender sprig muslin and yellow ribands, with a green cottage bonnet upon her crimped yellow curls, standing upon the doorstep, a hagridden

maid standing some paces behind her and looking as
if she wished herself far away.

"Russet," Lady Rockhall said.

"My lady," that august personage responded. There
had been bad blood between them since Russet had
relinquished his position at the house in order to continue with Lady Rockhall, and neither had quite forgotten the exchange.

Russet, with the merest hint of rudeness, awaited
her ladyship's commands.

"I," she proclaimed, "have come. You may announce
me to her ladyship. I shall attend her in the Green
Salon." She swept past the somewhat astonished butler
dragging the maid in her wake.

"Very good, madam," Russet murmured, deriving
some small sense of satisfaction from seeing her very
nearly collide with a footman bearing a carpet for the
hallway, as she closeted herself in this chamber.

Squaring his shoulders, Russet trod up the stairs to
the morning room, dark thoughts written clear upon
his countenance.

Miss Brandywine was holding a list in her hand
following her aunt about the room as the Dowager studied her wardrobe book. "Shall it be my emeralds with
my Paris green silk, or the sapphire and pearls with
my watered blue? But it has gold net and the sapphire
and pearl set are done in platinum—and I do not think
one should wear a tiara for a mere rout ball, do you?
Of course the mauve sarcenet, but that would mean
wearing my periodots, and they are quite dowdy—
Sophia was saying more to herself than her niece.

"...and I have sent word around to the constables
that we shall need a man to direct the carriages. In
Vienna, we always did so, and it saved a great row from
coachmen and linkboys over who had the right-of-
way..." Miss Brandywine was saying in her business-

like way. "The champagne of course, will come after the first set, and the orchestra leader has given me a list of his selections. Shall we have a first waltz, or shall we be content with a quadrille?"

"Of course I could wear my sarcenet gold, but I have always disliked that gown. Ought to have given it away long ago," Sophia murmured, absently pulling the ribands on her morning cap.

"...twenty to supper, if Charles manages to remember to come, I have sent a note around reminding him that he is obliged to be here no later than seven-thirty, so we shall have him by eight..." Miss Brandywine continued, reading from her list.

Russet burst upon this scene with rather more haste than he would have preferred. "Lady Rockhall is below, my lady," he announced in funereal tones. "She escorted herself to the Green Salon."

The effect was all that he could have wished for. Miranda's eyebrows shot upwards angrily, and Sophia pressed a hand to her bosom. "That Woman!" she said in tones of loathing. "Here?"

Russet bowed his head in assent.

"Hell-fire and brimstone!" Miranda exclaimed involuntarily, and cast an apologetic look at her aunt. But Sophia had not heard, though Russet might have murmured something that sounded rather like "exactly so, Miss."

Sophia was pulling herself up to her full, if somewhat neglible height. "That Woman, here! How dare she! Did you tell her I was not at home?"

"I had no opportunity, my lady. Lady Rockhall admitted herself to the Green Salon, and seems inclined to stay there until she sees you," Russet replied.

"How very like her! Odious female!"

"Aunt, you probably have no choice but to see her. Even Cousin Serena knows that no hostess would be

193

absent from her house when she is entertaining that evening."

"Where is Emily?" Sophia demanded.

"She was lying down upon her bed, the last I saw her," Miranda replied. "She has been a bit vaporish ever since I had my accident...you would think that it was she and not I who had..." She bit off the rest of her words, reminding herself that not everyone was as robust as she.

"I believe Miss Emily went out an hour ago, with the intention of strolling along the beach. I inquired if she wished a footman, but she replied that she did not wish to take anyone away from the preparations, and that she saw no impropriety in walking out alone in Sanditon," Russet supplied helpfully.

"Fortunate," Miranda said beneath her breath. "All we should need is Emily's hysterics, and you may depend upon it, Cousin Serena is exactly the person to produce them."

"Well! That Woman! I shall attend to her at once! Depend upon it, she has come to make mischief! Why Robert must marry that odious, toad-eating female! Miranda, come with me!"

"Indeed, Aunt! I should not want Cousin Serena to think that I was so lacking in manners as to not pay my respects," Miranda said drily.

Left to cool her heels in the Green Salon, Lady Rockhall had been occupying her time with running a glove over obscure surfaces in search of dust, and mentally estimating the cost of every item of the furnishings. She was fingering the nile green striped drapes (a guinea a yard if they had cost a shilling!) when her mother-in-law and cousin came into the room.

"Serena," Sophia said coolly. "What an unexpected surprise."

"Good day, Cousin Serena," Miranda echoed, clasping her hands at her waist and eyeing her cousin's *jeune toilette* with unconcealed astonishment.

Lady Rockhall bowed slightly. "How do you do, ma'am?" she asked Sophia with a cold smile, glancing at Miranda with an ancient dislike. "Ah, Miranda. I might have known. I thought you to be in Ghent or some other place."

"And I believed you to be at Hambly Court, Cousin Serena," Miss Brandywine replied.

"Do not be impertinent, Miranda. It was always one of your least becoming qualities."

Miranda looked as if she too wished to resume the old hostilities, but Sophia stepped into the breach. "To what do we owe the pleasure of this visit, Serena?" she inquired in the tone she might have used with a bothersome tradesman.

Sophia was treated to another display of her daughter-in-law's cold, toothy smile. "Not to put too fine a point upon it ma'am, I have come to take charge of my daughter. It is high time that she stopped these missish airs and settled to her duty. In short, I have selected a wedding date for her and Lord Marle, and she must come home and make ready for her marriage. Where is she?"

"Out walking," Sophia replied, and pressed her lips firmly together. "I do not know when to expect her back."

Lady Rockhall shook her head slightly. "Come now, ma'am. Even you cannot gainsay what Robert and I chose for our daughter. I am sure she has filled your head with missish tales about the viscount, but I assure you, he is in every way suitable. His position, his estates, his place in Society are all unimpeachable, and she should feel very fortunate to be making such a match. She will be a countess when the old earl finally passes on, and she had been a very, very naughty girl to run away from me like this."

"In short, Serena, Marle has every qualification for your toad-eating *ton*," her mother-in-law replied acidly.

Lady Rockhall's smile did not waver. "Lord Marle is in every way an excellent match for Emily, and she should be profoundly thankful that he offered for her. Why, Marle himself has come to Sanditon, I understand, though I have left my card several times upon Lady Denham, for some reason he has not been in touch with me." She raised her head slightly. "I know you, ma'am, and I know that you will indulge Emily's little fancies, but in this, I will brook no interference! Emily must marry Marle!"

"Even though they are as unsuited as oil and water?" Miranda interjected, forgetting herself. "Cousin Serena, you would sell your daughter to the highest bidder?"

"Watch your tongue, Miss, and recall to whom you speak," Lady Rockhall snapped, then recovering herself, smiled again her wintery smile. "Come now, Miranda, you have seen enough of the world to know that Emily must make a good match. And there could be none better than Marle!"

Miranda turned, barely controlling her temper. "None better! By God, ma'am, you would marry Emily, who is as innocent as a newborn, to a man who speaks of breaking her to bridle, an arrogant, overbearing, odious—oh!"

"I belive Miranda has stated my feelings, Serena, although she exaggerates slightly," Sophia said, eyes flashing. "As long as Emily wishes to remain beneath my roof, she will not marry where she does not wish!"

Whatever Lady Rockhall would have replied to this would never be known, for at that moment, Emily herself entered the room. Her leghorn hat was cast back from her face and hanging on its strings, and her cheeks were rosily flushed. For the first time in days, there was a glow of life about her. "Miranda, Russet said I should find you in here! I must—" she began, then broke off, staring at her mother as if she beheld a ghost. The color drained from her face and her mouth opened slightly.

"Emily, my dear," Lady Rockhall commanded. "Come and give your Mama a kiss."

Obediently, Emily crossed the room and placed her lips upon the rouged cheek presented to her. "Hullo, Mama," she said in a small voice.

"Very good," Lady Rockhall smiled. "Now what is all this foolishness about not wishing to marry Lord Marle? Your Papa and I have been quite vexed by your behavior, you know. Such a naughty little chit."

Emily opened and closed her mouth several times.

"Tell her, Emily," Miranda commanded.

"Yes, my little love," Lady Rockhall purred dangerously. "Tell me. It is all your cousin Miranda's doing, I have no doubt, filling you up with bluestocking notions and silly ideas. Your Gran'mama and your cousin have the idea in their heads that you do not wish to make a very good match with Lord Marle."

"I-I-" Emily struggled, clearly overcome with fear.

"Emily," Sophia said, "you do not have to marry anyone you do not wish to marry. You know that."

"Emily, my little love," her Mama purred, steel beneath velvet, "you have caused your Papa and I a great deal of trouble. And think of your poor sisters, who depend upon you! You would not wish to disappoint us, would you?"

Old habits die hard, and a lifetime spent beneath the domination of her mother in no way prepared Emily to deny her now. "I—" she stammered, quite overcome. She sank into a chair.

"How fortunate that you are entertaining tonight, dear ma'am," Lady Rockhall continued, twining her fingers into Emily's hair. "For I shall be able to announce to the world that I am betrothing my daughter to Lord Marle."

Sophia opened and closed her mouth.

"Emily!" Miranda said again, kneeling before her cousin and seizing both her hands in her own, "Look at me! Don't let her do this to you!"

"Only consider, my dear," Lady Rockhall cooed, "how very unpleasant it will be if you must return to Hambly Court an old maid! For I will not give you another season, and your sisters will all marry before you. You will be quite like Cousin Cordelia, you know."

"Nonsense! The girl will stay with me!" Sophia said militantly. "There will be time and time enough for her to find a suitable man, if she don't want Marle!"

"But she does want Marle, don't you, Emily?" Lady Rockhall purred. "Besides, ma'am, I might remind you that Emily is my daughter, and I have control over her until she is twenty-one! A merry scandal there would be—and believe me, I can make it very well known—if people were to find out the sort of cavorting you have condoned in your household! Oh, yes, Miranda, I know all about that young man of yours, and that inn—indeed, all of Sanditon knows that the three of you sepnt the night under one roof without so much as a chaperone! They'll hold their tongues as long as there's no one to start them thinking in quite another direction, but if I were to tell everyone what a hoyden you have always been, and how you've led my dear daughter astray—well, you see how it would be, do you not, Miranda? What will it be, Emily? Do you wish to quite ruin your own reputation and Miranda's, and discredit

198

your gran'mama, or will you come along peacefully? Marle could very easily cry off, you know, simply upon that head."

"Cousin Serena, you are the greatest beast in nature," Miranda cried. "You would not cut the reputation of your own daughter to shreds!"

Lady Rockhall gave her that dreadful smile, her eyes half-closed. "Well, Emily, will you marry Marle?"

"Don't do it!" Miranda cried.

Sophia looked as if she were about to have a stroke. Her face was beet red and her hands clenched and unclenched at her sides as if she wished, not for the first time, to strike her daughter-in-law down. "Serena," she said in awful tones, "I have known you to stoop low— to be absolutely ruthless in getting what you want— but I never thought even you could be so totally without principles!"

"But it is for Emily's own good," Lady Rockhall said smoothly.

"More for your own," Miranda could not help but retort.

Emily buried her head in her hands.

Russet chose that moment to throw open the door. "Lord Marle, my lady," he announced, and this time, he did lift one eyebrow in a very elegant gesture.

The viscount entered the room bearing three corsage boxes. "Good day, Lady Rockhall," he said, bowing toward her, "I did not mean to trouble you, but I wanted to present you all with flowers for tonight's—" He halted abruptly, took in the scene and cast a speaking look at Russet, who was just closing the doors behind him.

"Ah, Lord Marle!" Lady Rockhall said smoothly, all smiles again as she scurried to grasp his arm in the most familiar way. Marle's expression did not change, but he cast a look at her hand upon his arm.

"Good day, Lady Rockhall, an unexpected surprise to see you here," he said smoothly. "Sophia, I seem to have come at a bad time. Would you—"

"Oh, no, my lord," Lady Rockhall said swiftly. "Indeed, you could not have come at a better time. My little Emily has been a very, very naughty girl, I'm afraid, but now I have pointed out her error to her, and she is willing to agree to the date! How unfortunate that I should have missed you before this! It was my understanding that you were staying with Lady Denham, and I have left my card there several times without reply."

Marle took a step backward, removing Lady Rockhall's hand from his arm. "Been staying aboard my yacht, sorry to have missed you," he lied casually.

Lady Rockhall clicked her tongue. "Well, now, everything has been taken care of, and you may trust a wise mama will always bring matters to a successful head! Emily, do you not greet your fiancé?"

Miss Rockhall raised her face to Lord Marle's and tried to force a smile. Marle bowed before her.

"Tell Lord Marle that you are quite sorry, and that you will endeavor to conduct yourself properly in the future, Emily," Lady Rockhall said.

Emily repeated the words without much tone, and Marle inclined his head.

"And tell Lord Marle that you have consented to set the marriage date, and that we shall announce it tonight at your gran'mama's ball," Lady Rockhall pressed on.

Emily repeated this, also, looking at Marle as if she were facing her death.

Marle did not look at Miranda or Sophia. Very gravely, he nodded his head. "I am honored, Miss Rockhall," he said, bending over her. "May I present you with your corsage? I think you will find there is something to be said for the old-fashioned custom of the language of flowers."

Emily took the box from his hands and met his eyes for a single second before dropping them again into her lap. "Thank you," she whispered.

Lady Rockhall gave an unpleasant little laugh. "Well, I am so glad that is finally settled! Ah, Lord Marle, the guest list for the wedding will be quite *tonnish,* I assure you! Only the *crème de la crème* of the Upper Ten Thousand, you know! It shall be the event of the season, I hope!"

"Quite," Marle said quietly. "I am certain it will be talked of for days."

Emily made a little sound that Miranda thought was a sob, but since Miss Rockhall's head was still bowed over the corsage box, she could not see if she was crying. In an impotent fury, she regarded Marle with loathing. His arrogance, she fumed, blinded him to the reluctance of his bride.

"Well, now," Lady Rockhall sighed with relief. "My woman is upstairs packing your clothes, Emily. Now that I am here, you may come and stay in the Sanditon Hotel with me, so we may plan your trousseau. So much to do before the day arrives!" She gave her false little laugh. "We would, of course, stay with Sophia, Lord Marle, but Emily has imposed upon her dear gran'mama long enough. The Sanditon Hotel is an admirable establishment in its own way, or course, but hardly the sort of accommodations people of our station, Lord Marle, are used to."

Miranda made a strangled sound in the back of her throat, and received such an amused look from Marle that she yearned to slap him.

"Very good, ma'am," he told Lady Rockhall. "Perhaps you will do me the honor of allowing me to escort you and Emily to lunch there, since I happen to have some business in that direction. In an hour, perhaps?"

Lady Rockhall rustled her skirts. "So little time!" she chuckled. "That is, of course, Lord Marle, we should be delighted, should we not, Emily?"

"Yes, Mama," Emily said in a hollow voice, clutching the corsage box in her hands.

"Well then, perhaps we had best take leave. Say thank you to your gran'mama and to dear Cousin Miranda, and we shall be upon our way."

Miranda waited only until the door had closed upon the Rockhalls to rise from her chair. White with fury, she gave Marle a short bow. "If you will excuse me, sir," she said coldly, positively slamming the door behind her.

There were several pregnant seconds of silence after she had made her exit, during which Sophia regarded Lord Marle with an icy eye and he her with amusement writ upon his face.

Some words were exchanged before he took his leave of the Dowager and walked down the street toward the Strand whistling to himself and twirling his walking stick in a most unusually cheerful manner.

Sophia was closeted with her dresser when Miranda burst into the room, her small face white with fury. "That man! Cousin Serena!" she exclaimed, walking up and down and wringing her hands.

Sophia, having her hair brushed, leaned back in her chair and sighed. "Miranda, if you do not calm down instantly, you will be carried off with a stroke, exactly like Great-Uncle Trevor," she announced. "Or was it Cousin Ripley? I really cannot recall, except it had something to do with a footman disarranging his gout-stool, and it caused no end of trouble at the time."

Miranda stopped in mid-stalk and turned to look at

her aunt openmouthed. "How can you be so calm?" she demanded. "Aunt Sophia, it is entirely beyond reason! I should like to put a pistol to his head! Odious man! Monster! Ravisher of young females!"

Sophia opened one eye and regarded her niece. "Miranda Louisa Elizabeth—or is it Jane?—Brandywine, I will not have you in one of your tempers before my guests. Now calm down child! Nothing is so unsuitable to a female as to appear in company in a temper!"

"But, Aunt—"

Imperiously, Sophia raised a hand. "Miranda, it is nearly time to be dressed! Admiral Arkwright will be here at any moment, and he has steadfastly promised me that we shall have a look-in from the Duke of Clarence tonight, and whatever one may think of *him,* it is something in Sanditon to snare a Royal Duke!" She waved Miranda away. "Besides, I cannot believe that you would come through all those balls in Vienna without learning something of hiding your feelings. Are you, or are you not, Sir Francis's daughter?"

Miranda was indeed her father's daughter enough to be recalled to her military training, and in no good humor she betook herself off to submit to the ministrations of the capable Maria.

But, it must be added that she had a great deal of relief in venting her foul temper upon this imperious person in a rousing trilingual battle in which the Portuguese woman roundly bested her by reminding her that her last temper tantrum had resulted in her giving her notice, a memory which quickly made Miranda capitulate. Defeat, she reminded herself, also demanded dignity, and she haughtily submitted to Maria's efforts in a proud silence.

Despite all, the redoubtable Maria was able to send her mistress downstairs to greet the first dinner guests as a credit to her own profession. A somewhat sulky countenance by no means diminished the perfection of Miss Brandywine's toilette. Her dark curls had been brushed into a méduse, and a cord of sapphire blue had been wound through her tresses, held with a clip of white roses above one ear. In her ears, Maria had fastened the set of pearl and diamond drops Sir Francis had presented his daughter upon her eighteenth birthday, and about her neck, she wore a long length of pearls and diamonds, turned twice. Her ball dress had seen two Viennese parties and had received many compliments, for it was of a sea-blue shade of watered silk with an overslip of silver gauze, trimmed with embroidered stripes of white roses nestled among green leaves, and banded about the cap sleeves and deep hem with ruchings of pointe-pois lace. Upon her feet she wore thin sandals of rose silk, and over one arm Maria had placed a Vienna shawl of the deep sapphire hue that set Miranda off to advantage.

Sophia, in her claret satin and rose ball gown, a headdress of blush feathers placed upon her curls and the full complement of her late mother's diamonds upon ears, neck, wrists and bosom, sailed majestically out of her boudoir to join her niece upon the stairs, her train hitched over one arm. She cast an approving eye over her niece and nodded serenely as her dresser adjusted one of the small plumes before allowing her to leave her hands.

"I should like very much to have the headache," Miranda said sulkily to her aunt as they descended the stairs together.

Sophia turned a diamond bracelet around her wrist. "As your Papa would say, we may have lost the war, but not the battle—or is it the other way around? For Lord's sake, child, do try to put a good face upon it— ah, Henry, how wonderful of you to come," she exclaimed, extending her hand to Admiral Arkwright, who was gazing up at her from the bottom of the stairs with unconcealed admiration.

Lord Marle, resplendent in his somber evening black, and to Miranda's eye, even more incongruous than ever in formal dress, abandoned Lady Denham to her hostess in order to bend over Miranda's hand. "Ravishing," he said simply. "Do you save me a waltz, Miss Brandywine?"

"My card is filled," Miranda said stiffly.

Lord Marle plucked it from her hand and cast an eye down its spaces. "Should not be dancing upon that ankle of yours at all, you know! and yet, despite all, I do see a space here. The second waltz, Miss Brandywine?" He scrawled his name across the line and returned her the card, with a look she could have sworn was a wink. "Never lie outright when a half truth will do, you know," he said as he turned away to bow to Sophia.

Miranda glared at him back with daggers in her eyes, but at that moment, she was distracted by the arrival of Lady Rockhall in an unbecoming shade of pastel pink and a very unsavory look of triumph about her. Beneath her rouge, her cheeks were flushed and her eyes glittered as she seized upon Lord Marle's arm in a proprietary way.

Miranda made a move toward Emily, breathlessly beautiful in a simple dancing dress of ivory silk overlaid with a net of silver gauze, her flaxen tresses curled *à la aphrodite* upon her head and allowed to fall in gentle curls about her face. In contrast to the furbelows and ribands of her mother's dress, nothing could have been more appealing than her simplicity, and her only ornament, a single strand of pearls, set off her ethereal paleness to perfection. There were dark circles in the hollows of her cheeks, and her eyes, when she looked at Miranda, seemed to have a half-hysterical glint in them. Seeing her cousin, Emily started toward her, but Lady Rockhall, with a look of purest hatred at Miranda, grasped her daughter's arm and gave her a slight push in the direction of Lord Marle, all the while speaking in the most odiously caressing manner.

Miranda started toward her cousin, but was interrupted by Lady Denham, who, in her frank way, complimented Miranda's dress and demanded to know if it was all the fashion in Europe now for young ladies to wear such a low decolletage. Emily was soon lost from Miranda's sight as other guests arrived and demanded her attention, and she was forced to smile and respond politely, all the while experiencing an inner torment that would have delighted the demons of hell.

Her temper was by no means calmed when Mr. Hartley put in his carelessly rumpled appearance only a few minutes before Russet announced dinner.

"Miranda," he said rather breathlessly, taking her fingers into his own and looking at her from the depths of his pale blue eyes. "Forgive me—"

"Oh, don't bother!" she snapped, extending her bad temper to her fiancé. "Honestly, Charles, I wonder where you leave your mind at times. You are never there when I need you the most! That witch of a mother of Emily's has shown up on the scene and simply destroyed everything in the most unbelievable fashion. And, I would like to know, where have you been when I needed you the most? Charles, it is really too bad of you! I—I begin to think that we will not suit, this way!"

Charles pushed a hand through his Byronic curls. "Miranda, if only you would listen to me—" he began.

At that moment, Russet sounded the dinner gong, and Charles escorted her to dinner.

Placed between a very deaf old gentleman and a naval officer who seemed more interested in his food than conversation, Miranda sipped at her wine and picked at course after course of Alphonse's highest art. At least, she thought as the naval officer accepted a third helping of curried sole, someone appreciated the chef's heroic efforts. *Venaison aux amandes* was removed for *poule rôtie* with a remove of oyster pie, and each time she heard Lady Rockhall's laugh, Miranda had to fight down the urge to scream. Watching Emily down the table, picking listlessly at her own plate, two fiery spots of color in her cheeks set out against her pale skin, Miranda wanted to cry. Marle, seated at Sophia's left, however, seemed to be eating with good appetite and witty conversation, for she heard her aunt's laugh once or twice, and even caught her slapping the viscount's arm playfully with her fan.

Miranda twisted her napkin in her lap and considered Mr. Hartley almost directly across from her, chewing thoughtfully and gazing into a space somewhere above the footman's head while a stout dowager on his left and a young miss on his right both gazed at him with the adoration they might accord Adonis.

But Miranda, in her sulks, saw him in a different light, and by the time *gâteux au chocolat avec crème brulée* had been removed untouched from her place and substituted with an arrangement of strawberries and india-sugar, it was as if she were regarding a stranger. How had she come to get engaged to him? she wondered in some astonishment, noting his hair needing combing and his cravat had a spot of soup. Even to herself, her train of thought became unreadable, and the idea that she had ever considered a lifetime with Mr. Charles Hartley—had it been Viennese madness?—seemed as alien to her as life upon the moon.

It seemed as if Sophia would never rise from the table, giving the ladies the signal to leave the gentlemen to their port and cigars, and when, after what seemed to Miranda to be ages, she finally did, her niece did not join the other ladies directly, but retired to her own room to indulge in an activity that left her eyes suspiciously red-rimmed when she rejoined the guests.

The ball was about to start, and custom dictated that she take her place beside her aunt to receive those who had been invited. But even here, there was no space for as much as a look with Emily, for Cousin Serena asserted herself firmly between the two girls in such a manner that Miranda's teeth were set on edge. Custom, of course, dictated her place there, but even Sophia raised an eyebrow at the way in which her daughter-in-law fawned upon the more illustrious of the guests, recalling a chance meeting or a conversation in passing as the excuse to claim an intimate friendship with those who were hard pressed to recall her name.

Lady Rockhall had spent half her lifetime attempting to storm the highest reaches of the *ton,* and tonight, with the promise of one of its most popular members as an addition to her family, she postively crowed in her triumph.

Miranda was far too polite to squirm visibly at Lady Rockhall's coy hints and sallies, but she was thankful that she was placed between her cousin and her aunt so that lady was spared the worst of her daughter-in-law's snares and simpering hints. Miss Brandywine, who by no stretch of the imagination could be labeled a high stickler or a snob, counted her intimates for their merits rather than their rank or position, and nothing could be more repulsive to her than an individual who weighed others solely upon their value to her own social ambitions.

Therefore, although she did not feel in the least like dancing, she was relieved when Mr. Hartley claimed her hand for the opening quadrille—at least it meant an escape from Cousin Serena's endless "My dear Lady . . . Oh, but we are quite bosom-beaux, Lord . . ."

Taking her place in the set with Charles, she was aware of Emily and Marle forming the other half of their dance. Charles, never the best of dancers, looked vaguely uncomfortable; Emily was trembling like a leaf; Marle, easily graceful for so rough a man, had that singularly irritating smile upon his face.

The music started, and they began to move through the old-fashioned, formal steps.

Turn, step, step, step, dip, step, bow. Miranda curtseyed to Charles, bowed and turned again, watching the floor filling with dancers.

"Miranda," Charles said. "I must speak with you."

"And I with you—"

Miranda turned away again and met Marle, placing her hand on top of his. Step, slide, step, and turn. "I hope you are satisfied," she said through clenched teeth.

"Very," he replied, bowing as she dropped a curtsey.

"You—" Turn again, and she was facing Charles.

"Miranda, something has happened. It affects us."

"Indeed, Charles, it does! I know not how to say this, but—"

Turn again, step and slide, and she had a glimpse of Emily's face as she faced Charles and he took her hand for the round.

"Miss Brandywine, pay attention or you will ruin my shoes!" Lord Marle said as she faced him, giving him both her hands and pointing her toe.

"Rather you will ruin my slippers! Are you so blind that you cannot see that poor chit is terrif—"

She caught only a hint of Marle's elusive smile as they bowed and turned again.

"Charles, you really must not think that I—"

"Miranda, you are the most estimable of women, you will always be a goddess to me, but—"

Turn, step, and curtsey and she was facing Emily.

"My dearest cousin, you must forgive me—" Miss Rockhall said a little breathlessly.

"It is I who must be forgiven, Emily! To back down from Cousin Serena!" Miranda said, turning away again to face Lord Marle. She slid her hand on top of his and they promenaded the floor.

"Only a monster of the most selfish, unfeeling instincts could behave as you have!" she hissed, not looking at him.

"Do you think so? I thought myself rather clever."

Miranda almost stopped in her tracks, but Marle led her inexorably on. "Have a care, or we shall collide into His Grace! Do you see Admiral Arkwright? In his full-dress uniform with all those medals, he resembles nothing so much as a naval Romeo Coates!"

Despite herself, Miranda was distracted. She actually giggled, before she recalled herself. "You are abominable, sir!"

She was facing Charles again. "Abominable?" he asked. "Yes, yes, I am—but Miranda, please, you must understand—"

"No, no, it is you that must understand, Charles. It will not fadge! Oh, I cannot—you are estimable, Charles, and wonderfully romantic and—"

"Romantic?" Lord Marle asked as he faced her. "I would not say it was romantic, precisely, she has a very good idea of the burdens she will have to bear—"

"Then why do you persist in this course?" Miranda demanded, step, step, step, slide and turn. "Surely, an unwilling bride can give you no pleasure—" Turn, and curtsey.

"No pleasure at all, Miranda, that is why you must—

210

most wonderful Miranda, be strong!" Charles said, bowing to her.

"But it is more than I can endure to see!" Miranda replied. "He is not—fit to marry—" Turn again, and face Lord Marle.

The dance ended as Miranda sank into a curtsey and Marle taking her hand, bowed over it. As she rose, her eyes met his. All about them, the dancers were applauding, but Miranda felt as if the ballroom were a great distance away, as if she and Marle were alone. Slowly, and without taking his eyes from her own, Marle raised her hand to his lips and lightly kissed it.

"The second waltz, Miss Brandywine," the viscount repeated, as his partner was seized by an enthusiastic young man with military mustaches.

Set after set passed, and Miranda did not lack for partners who were solicitous of her injured ankle, and just as anxious to share a moment with her in a secluded alcove as they were to spin her about the floor. She drank champagne and ate an oyster patty; out of long habit, she forced herself to laugh and to make what she hoped would pass for witty conversation and drolleries. With a great deal of effort, she forced herself not to stare after Marle on the ballroom floor, or give Lady Rockhall any sense of satisfaction by watching her progress with a reluctant Royal Duke; all the world knew Clarence must marry a fortune to pay his enormous debts, and furthermore, the polite world tended to look askance upon the Royal Dukes anyway, so let her have the old man. Upon being presented to this remarkable individual, she was a little astonished at the way in which his corsets creaked alarmingly loud as he bent over her hand and inquired very politely after his old friend Sir Francis, but even as she fetched up witty gossip from Vienna for His Grace's edification, she kept half an eye upon the ballroom floor, looking for Emily, who must, she was certain, be near hysterics by this time.

Although her fortune was adequate, perhaps even ample, it was hardly enough to attract the impoverished Duke, and therefore Miranda must feel that is was sheer force of her personality that kept him chattering to her for above ten minutes. But, feeling that she had rewarded this august gentleman's time with several very good Viennese *on dits,* she was relieved when Admiral Arkwright abjured his old crony to make for the card room for a rubber or two of whist at ten-pound points. Feeling that she had ascertained the reason for His Grace's need to dangle after heiresses, Miss Brandywine gave him her best bow and breathed a sigh of relief.

But if she hoped to find Emily, she was disappointed, for there was no sight of her upon the floor, nor did she see any glimpse of Mr. Hartley.

She was about to make inquiries of Sophia when Marle appeared from (it seemed) thin air, and bowed before her. "My waltz, I believe, Miss Brandywine," he said smoothly, and before she could make any demur, had his arm firmly about her waist and was leading her into the floor.

"Now, Miss Brandywine, a word with you," the viscount said, spinning her about in time to the music.

"No, my lord! First, a word with you, if you please!" Miranda snapped.

Something twitched at the corners of his mouth, but he inclined his head. "Very well, ma'am! But only if you do not try to lead!"

Miranda bit her lip and was silenced for several seconds. But seconds only. "Lord Marle," she began ponderously, "someone *must* tell you! Emily has not the courage, Lady Rockhall has far too much tact, and Charles—well, Charles is—"

"Charles," he finished for her. She shot him a look from beneath her lashes and he inclined his head. "Pray continue."

Miranda took a deep breath. "Lord Marle, Emily does not wish to marry you! In fact, you terrify her! My cousin is, by nature, a shy, withdrawn person who has always led a quiet life! Her nature is such that those of stronger personality may easily bully her—as her Mama does most mercilessly! Lord Marle, the sort of life you lead is—is totally unsuitable for my cousin! She is no more equipped to hostess Runford Place than a babe in a cradle! Sailing makes her seasick, and she is afraid of horses! And you—you affright her dreadfully with your abrupt manners and your cynicism and your arrogance! All of these traits may be put down to your family background, and you may be excused from them, but only consider—" Miranda broke off, frowning at his smile. "What in the name of cannon fire made you chose a girl barely out of the schoolroom in the first place?"

Marle shrugged lightly. "I had to marry. I am approaching thirty, Miss Brandywine, and my father, after a life spent in what can only be considered riotous debauchery—"

"Mad Jack Runford," Miranda put in.

"Exactly so, Mad Jack put the screws to me! M'father and I are not upon the best of terms, you see! The source of our disagreements is the way in which he has illmanaged our estates these many years. Well, to make a long story short, Miss Brandywine—I do not wish to bore you—we laid a wager. I would have control of our land before he ruined us all if I would agree to produce an heir before he was burnt to the socket! Harebrained scheme, I know, but most women bore me to death, with their simpering airs and their die-away 'la, sirs'. So, I thought if I must marry, then I shall choose a female who can be molded to the compliance to the ideals I wanted. So, I chose Miss Rockhall. She did not seem adverse to my suit—she knew there was no love involved, and I believed that she considered my title and my position adequate recompense for her disdain of my person. I did not know until much later that her Mama was behind her, pulling her strings like a puppet!"

Miranda looked thoughtful, but said nothing.

"When I found that she had fled Hambly Court and come to her grandmother's in Sanditon, I knew there was something amiss. I didn't quite believe Lady Rockhall's stories about exhaustion and Emily pining away for me, and I wanted to see her without her Mama to attempt to ascertain that she was, indeed, willing to marry her. But you, Miss Brandywine, never gave me the chance to see Emily alone! Whenever I thought to seize a moment with her, you were there. Protecting her, I have no doubt, from my advanced lechery!"

Miranda bit her lip.

"So, you see, Miss Brandywine, you have interfered for naught! Had I only been able to have a moment alone with Emily at the beginning, it would have been all over in a trice. But you, with your managing ways, have led us all such a merry chase that after a time it amused me to see what you would think of next!"

"Then you do not wish to marry Emily either! Oh, that is the most famous thing!" Miranda exclaimed. "We must tell her at once! You have no idea of what sort of blackmail my Cousin Serena has exerted upon us all this day! Lord, I shall love to see the look on her face—"

"You shall have that pleasure soon enough," Marle promised her.

"But where is Emily? I do not see her—or Charles—not that Charles—" She craned her neck about the

214

oom. "Cousin Serena—she will make her announce-
ent—you must stop her! Marle!"

"Easy, my little busybody," Lord Marle laughed.
For once, Miranda Brandywine, someone else has
aken all the managing out of your hands!"

"Whatever do you mean?" Miranda asked, rather
rmly being kept in the time of the waltz by Lord
Marle.

"You shall see, in just a moment. I believe Sophia
s approaching the orchestra leader now."

And indeed, that lady was sailing majestically across
he floor all claret and rose and diamonds, her train
weeping across the floor. From her corner, Lady Den-
am was watching with a very satisfied smile upon her
ace.

As the dance ended, Sophia climbed the dais, raising
er arms for attention.

From the corner where she had buttonholed a par-
cularly important dowager marchioness, Lady Rock-
all turned, uneasiness written upon her face.

"Your attention please! May I have your attention
lease! I wish to make a very happy and very important
nnouncement!" Sophia called, and all eyes turned ex-
ectantly upon her. She clasped her glittering hands
gainst her stomacher and smiled. "I am pleased to
nnounce that my niece, Miss Miranda Louisa Eliza-
eth—or is it Jane?—Brandywine is betrothed to Vis-
ount Marle!"

Miranda stood thunderstruck while applause and
ongratulations rained down upon her. She was dimly
ware of Marle smiling at her in that odd way of his,
imly aware of Lady Rockhall's pale face contorted
ith fury, the twin spots of rouge in her cheeks alight
ke beacons as she stalked out of the ballroom. Almost
ysterically, she looked about for some sight of Charles
r Emily, but people—so many people were thinging

215

about her, wishing to kiss her cheek or shake her hand or clap Marle upon the back or say a word that she barely knew how she stayed upon her feet.

Only when the orchestra had struck up the strains of a country dance did the fervor subside somewhat. Still in a state of shock, she allowed Marle to guide her off the floor toward a little balcony overlooking the garden.

He handed her a glass of champagne and she drained it down in one gulp, before facing him, her face strangely expressionless. But she had that look in her eye, and Marle quickly grasped her wrist.

"I don't want champagne in my face any more than I want to sprain your wrist again."

"How could you—all those people! Your little jokes, Marle, are neither harmless nor amusing!" Miranda flared.

"Charmingly exasperating!" He smiled.

"What am I to say to Charles! Or Emily! What must they think of me! Of you?"

"I don't think you will have to worry about facing them, not for a while, anyway. You see, Emily and Charles were married this morning by special license."

Miranda froze, staring at Marle in total incomprehension.

"That is correct, Miss Brandwyine. This morning by special license, at St. Murdo's in Old Sanditon. Myself and the vicar's wife were the witnesses."

"She said she was walking on the beach—" Miranda murmured. "And then, she came in and—Good God Cousin Serena was there! And you knew all along and said nothing! Marle you are a wretch!"

"Are you terribly hurt? I may not be very much, by contrast to the poetic Mr. Hartley, but if you had not been so busy throwing those two together these past two months, and trying to bait me on every turn of the

216

road, you might have noticed that they are very much in love."

"Emily and Charles. Good God," Miranda said, stunned.

"Exactly so. Emily and Charles."

"Cousin Serena will rend her limb from limb! Charles has nothing! Only that cottage in Hampshire!"

"On the contrary, Mr. Hartley will soon be a warm man. No nabob, I assure you, but the patent upon his navigational depth-finding device will no doubt make him a good annuity! The Navy has been looking for such an instrument for years, and Charles had the genius to perfect it! Well, I helped him a bit, of course, but still and all, it was his idea and his work. I think Miss Rockhall and Mr. Hartley will manage quite happily, when they return from their honeymoon."

"Honeymoon?"

"Yes. France. I lent them the use of my yacht for the crossing. Even Lady Rockhall cannot dash off in hot pursuit to France, you know. And I imagine by the time they return, she will be reconciled."

"Emily—and Charles!" Miranda repeated, shaking her head. "What a fool I have been." She raised her head slightly. "They will deal together very well, I think, do not you? Lord, if I had married Charles, what a merry dance I would have led him! We both would have been miserable within a twelvemonth."

"As much as Emily and I would have been."

"Why didn't you tell me?" Miranda demanded. "Why didn't someone tell me? Lord, what I must have done!"

"Precisely why I did not tell you," Marle said. "You would have managed us all into an even worse tangle! If I had not plied Hartley with wine and pried the whole tale out of him, they would have spent the rest of their lives, married miserably to us, always yearning for each other, and never quite summoning the courage to consummate their guilty passions."

"It sounds absolutely ghastly," Miranda said drily. She put a hand to her cheek. "Oh, Lord, Emily and Charles! It is too perfect, is it not? And you contrived it all! And you told me you were no gentleman! Marle, I suspect that beneath that cynical, arrogant exterior, there must lie a heart as soft as porridge!"

"That, my dear, Miss Brandywine, will be our little secret. Anyway, I do not envy Charles his seasick bride on that Channel crossing. Doubtless she shall inspire an ode to *mal de mer!*"

"Good God," said Miss Brandywine, thoroughly appalled. "And no doubt Emily shall think it deathless verse!" She shook her head. "Perfect! Simply perfect! Outmanned, outflanked, outgunned and taken in ambush!"

"Then you will surrender?"

"Never!" Miss Brandywine said firmly. "Lord Marle, you need not marry me because you have spirited away my fiancé, you know."

"Then you must consider, Miss Brandywine, that you have robbed me of a fiancée, deliberately and with malice aforethought! I must need have a wife, and there seems to be no other female."

Miranda leaned against the stone rail of the balcony and crossed her arms over her chest, regarding the viscount steadily. "This is true. But you know, Marle, I ought to say not simply to embarrass you after making Aunt say that piece, without so much as a by-your-leave."

"Ah," Marle leaned back against the opposite rail and thrust his hands into his pockets. "But if I had come up to you and said, 'Miss Brandywine, your fiancé has just eloped with my fiancée, will you marry me,' you would have said no."

218

Miranda considered this. "You are correct."

"This way, you have no choice. You have to marry me, Miranda. Miranda! How well they named you! Everywhere you go, you stir up a tempest!"

"Vincent is not such a very bad name, either. I wonder if I could become used to sitting across the breakfast table from a man named Vincent?"

"Vincent George Gore St. John Christopher, to be precise. You'd better say you'll marry me, Miranda Brandywine. I doubt there's another female in Christendom who could stand up to m'father's gout tempers."

"Sir Francis will doubtless approve of you," Miss Brandywine said thoughtfully. "And that would be quite a change. He has never approved of my beaux."

"If they've all been like poor Hartley, not bloody likely!"

"Aunt approves of you," Miranda mulled thoughtfully.

"Lady Denham has long said that you were the only female for me."

They leaned back against their railings in comfortable silence, regarding each other for some space of time.

"I am very managing. I have a beastly temper and I tend to talk in military cant. *And*, Lord Marle, I am a firm believer in the rights of females."

"I, Miss Brandywine, am no gentleman. I am arrogant, ruthless, cynical and believe that a woman's place is in the home."

"Would it be a breakfast table on a pitching ship, sometimes?" Miranda asked a little wistfully.

"A pitching ship, an African jungle, a dining table for twenty, sometimes in the saddle, if you wish. But always side to side, Miranda, always toe to toe."

"It would never be dull, would it?"

"Never, I have a feeling, would it be dull."

"There is only one other thing, Marle. It is trivial, but I think worth bringing up."

"Indeed, Miranda. And what would that be?"

"Love." Miranda replied.

Marle pushed himself lightly off the balustrade and advanced upon Miranda. Miss Brandywine was pleased to think that she gave as good as she got, and besides, Lord Marle smelled of clean linen and leather, quite pleasantly masculine. She rested her head against his chest and sighed, content.

"Love," Marle said firmly, and proceeded to give Miranda a second demonstration.

ABOUT THE AUTHOR

Rebecca Baldwin is the *nom de plume* of a rather modest lady who makes her home on the Eastern Shore of Maryland and spends part of each year in England. Under other aliases, she has published mysteries, fantasies and a work on the occult. She has completed her first contemporary novel and is at work upon her second. This is her ninth historical romance as Rebecca Baldwin. She reads tarot cards, Raymond Chandler, Eudora Welty, and, of course, Jane Austen.

Let COVENTRY Give You
A Little Old-Fashioned Romance

FAWCETT COLUMBINE
COOKBOOKS

Illustrated, specialty cookbooks in large format.

☐ THE CHICKEN COOKBOOK   90049 $6.95
By Sophie Kay and The Editors of Consumer Guide ®
Still one of the most economical and nutritious foods, chicken is also one of the most versatile. This book contains over 200 recipes as well as storage tips, cooking hints and nutritional information.

☐ CONVECTION OVEN COOKBOOK   90042 $6.95
By Beatrice Ojakangas and The Editors of Consumer Guide ®
Over 200 tasty, easy to follow recipes for broiling, roasting, baking, slow-cooking and dehydrating. Also includes a section on conversion of conventional oven recipes to convection oven.

☐ THE FOOD INFLATION FIGHTER'S
HANDBOOK   90030 $5.95
By Judith L. Klinger
A comprehensive guide on beating the high cost of food. This book is filled with useful tips on saving money; from shopping to entertaining. Also includes money-saving recipes.

☐ THE NEW YORK TIMES 60-MINUTE
GOURMET   90045 $6.95
By Pierre Franey
Gourmet recipes that can be prepared in an hour or less. Includes nearly 300 recipes for main dishes as well as appropriate accompanying side dishes.

☐ THE WOMAN'S DAY GREAT AMERICAN
COOKIE BOOK   90032 $5.95
Edited by Julie Houston
An original collection of best-loved cookies from *Woman's Day* magazine. Over 250 recipes which include useful tips on substitutions, storing and freezing.

Buy them at your local bookstore or use this handy coupon for ordering.

COLUMBIA BOOK SERVICE (a CBS Publications Co.)
32275 Mally Road, P.O. Box FB, Madison Heights, MI 48071

Please send me the books I have checked above. Orders for less than 5 books must include 75¢ for the first book and 25¢ for each additional book to cover postage and handling. Orders for 5 books or more postage is FREE. Send check or money order only.

Cost $_____	Name _____
Sales tax*_____	Address _____
Postage_____	City _____
Total $_____	State _____ Zip _____

The government requires us to collect sales tax in all states except AK, DE, MT, NH and OR.

This offer expires 1 February 82   8169

FAWCETT COLUMBINE

HUMOR

America's favorite comic strips in large-format cartoon books.

☐ B.C. COLOR ME SUNDAY   90004 $5.95
By Johnny Hart
The escapades of a most delightful cave-man.

☐ DRABBLE   90052 $3.95
By Kevin Fagan
The touching but hilarious foibles of college studen
Norman Drabble.

☐ ON VACATION WITH THE
FAMILY CIRCUS   90006 $4.95
By Bil Keane
Join the family on vacation as the kids drive Mom
and Dad crazy.